Realms of Lust and Love

E.B. WILD

Any and all comments, questions, or concerns are very welcomed to contact
ebwildbooks@gmail.com

ISBN: 9798456569752

"Love is the one thing we're capable of perceiving that transcends dimensions of time and space. Maybe we should trust that, even if we can't understand it"
—Dr. Amelia Brand

Interstellar by Christopher Nolan

CHAPTER 1

Elle sat in her car with the engine idling, its fumes emanating smoke into the night, she looked down at her phone unsure of her next move. She was fixated on the blank text message screen with that persistent pulsating line, just taunting her. The soft blue light reflected off her face and created a deeper contrast on her eyebrows, revealing her uncertainty. She knew that if she contacted him, all her old feelings for him would resurface almost instantaneously.

It's been a couple of months since they have spoken, but his presence was constantly felt. She inhaled through her nose deeply and looked up for a moment, peering into the still night. Elle pondered all the outcomes that would result if she sent him a message, and ultimately decided against it all.

She thought it was best to just shut the car off and go home. She glanced down again at her phone, at that pulsating line just blinking on and off as if it knew something had to be said. Something about that vertical cursor that drew her in, seemed to be alive and impatient. It was waiting for the right words just as she had been waiting to see him again.

At that moment her fingers typed and sent a message before she was able to second guess herself. "Where are you? Are you free tonight?"

There it was again, the pulsating vertical cursor that had nothing left to say, it remained only to taunt her. It blinked at the same rate as her heartbeat did, which after close inspection, Elle deemed it to be at a calmer tempo than what she expected. She was upset, furious, disappointed, and confused. She had not seen Don in weeks.

This would not have been an issue otherwise except for the fact that they were meeting constantly every two days. Like clockwork, every two days he would reach out to her, and they would meet. It has been just over three weeks now and she had heard nothing from him. There were no indications that anything was off, it all seemed to be going swimmingly, yet she had heard nothing from him. Not one word. She was keeping calm and collected, but only because to not do so, would result in her just panicking, and probably chucking her phone. Then how would she—

"I am. Go through the AP and come to me," the text came in, interrupting her thoughts. She read the text message out loud but heard only his voice. His voice was ingrained in her head by now, periodically appearing and reminding her words of encouragement. But tonight, was different.

She would get to hear his voice in real-time, and not just in her mind. Elle reached over into her glove compartment and started shuffling through old gadgets and paperwork, allowing most of it to fall onto the seat and the floor. She started to think that she might have misplaced the Wrist-Vector Don had given her a few weeks ago. Then she realized it was not there, it was in the overhead compartment.

She pulled the lever open and it fell right onto her lap. She held it in her palm for a moment, rubbing the pyramid crystal centerpiece as if it was his hand that was there instead, then latched it secured to her wrist. She turned off her phone and shifted her car into drive. A smile arose out the right corner of her mouth as she drove into the night towards him.

CHAPTER 2

D on began his night by pouring himself a glass of homemade moonshine. No matter how many times he went to revisit home planet Earth, he could never find a drink that could top this local brew. Tonight, he especially longed for a tall glass filled to the rim with ice. As of late, it was only for special occasions that he would reach into the fridge, but just for a single ice cube. Mostly, his ice reserve was for when he had company over. Lately, his company had only been lost strangers stumbling by once every few months or so. The energy supplied to his humble abode was used primarily to keep his communications and navigational equipment on and updated as much as possible. After all, that was going to be the only way he could plot a course back to Earth, once enough material was gathered to reconstruct his Wrist-Vector. He had been living there consecutively now for about 2 years, and still had no clue if he was close to his return. What started as a research journey, quickly turned into a daily fight to survive, and now he has adapted and has made Joshua Hills Waypoint his new home. This world that he was stranded in was not much of a world at all, rather a waypoint. At least that's what the knowledge books called it. It took some time for Don to establish his residence here. Luckily, he found the right locals who were done with their time at this waypoint and graciously handed over the abode to him after years of working off his rent.

As he paced over to his balcony with a drink in hand, he laid his eyes upon the sea of doors, all individually inserted into the ground. The ground itself was mostly barren, just patches of grass here and there, only appearing sporadically across the dirt-filled land. The endless horizon of doors always placed him in awe. There were just so many doors, and all the doors in this waypoint led to other worlds, in other dimensions and realms. There were so many doors here, much more than Don ever imagined there would be. During his studies, this waypoint was of utter fascination to him, and he knew he would visit. What made this waypoint so unique was that the doors shifted, and crawled into different locations every night. The only way he knew which ones he had already been through was by lightly marking them with his blade.

Unexpectedly, his communication system lit up and glowed green, indicating he was receiving a transmission. Questionable to have a signal come in this late. The only signals he usually received that late were from glitching tech drones that have recently crashed. With his interest peaked, he finished his drink and walked over to his TeleQuik comm-system. There against the green screen that took over the entire wall read a simple message "Where are you? Are you free tonight?" Don read it and knew instantly it was from Elle. He stared at the message and wondered how long it has been since he had seen her. Time worked differently in Joshua Hills Waypoint; it went faster. For Elle, it's only been a few weeks since their last meeting, yet he knew it had to be at least two years for him. So much has happened since then, his heart has grown colder, his body has added more scars, and his mind had lost a few more screws. He peered into the message as if searching for her face, and then it appeared in his mind. Her soft caramel skin and curly buoyant hair. He could now see clearly her plump lips, smiling as they always did when she looked at him, and it reminded him that he was still very much a part of existence. He then thought of her ridiculously large eyes that pierced right through to his soul. He then heard her voice, with no words in particular but just humming in his mind. Don began to hum along. He was glad that he was capable of still missing someone, then he realized that he missed her at that very moment more than he expected to. That was all that he needed to know in order to respond.

He replied to her.

Don then walked over to cold storage, picked an ice cube, and placed it into his glass. While walking back to the balcony, he grabbed the bottle of Moonshine and refilled his drink. He stared once again over the horizon of doors, yet the sight was not filled with awe now, it held anticipation and hope. It was now all up to Elle to find him. It was up to her to use the techniques he taught her to navigate through the portals and reach him.

CHAPTER 3

I t took Elle some time to realize that she had been driving in complete silence. Her mind was filled with conversations that would take place. She pondered on what would be the first words out of her mouth, and what would be the first words out of his. She went further into her own head and visualized them just standing in front of each other speechless.

And Naked. Words and body parts just floating in her mind as she drove down the highway. There was no room for the music to be playing from her speakers, her mind was too engaged. It wasn't until she drove over the rumble strips on the side of the highway lane that she realized she was too deep in thought and should reprioritize her focus. She lowered her driver-side window and turned the radio on. Static. She was too far from the city limits; no frequencies would reach her there. She contemplated pulling over and searching for her outdated CDs, but realized that would not be necessary since her Wrist-Vector began to judder intermittently.

She was close now. She had to be alert and pay attention or else she could miss the subtle clues. She began to hear his voice again now, hear his words describing all the clues and the path to take to Joshua Hills Waypoint. It was Don that introduced her to this area a year ago, and it was also the first time that she had been sexually intimate with him. Their passionate endeavors constantly led them to explore new areas, yet these sacred lands called Joshua Hills were a part of history that only Don knew about from his studies. She began to recollect her first time here before she knew of the portals and doors.

The Before time.

Don had taken her to Joshua Hills in order to show her that there was more than the city life she grew up in. The city stretched vast and further than most in the world, yet it was not the only thing. To Elle however, it was the only thing she had known. She met Don while working as a nurse in the city's second most prestigious hospital. He came in to have blood drawn and tested. At first, he was nothing but another patient, but what stood out was his tattoo. As she prepped him to draw blood, she couldn't help but get drawn into it. His tattoo spanned from his left shoulder to just past his elbow and was intricately detailed with planets of all types of shapes, and colors. She even thought it was moving until she realized it was just him flexing his triceps a bit. Don chuckled as Elle realized it was just him messing with her. She teasingly slapped him on his arm which was quite out of character for her. She immediately began to apologize as he chuckled only harder and placed his hand on hers. "It's okay, it's okay, I know." Elle felt gravitated to his laughter, and she laughed along. She could feel his laughter as if it was emanating from her own vocal cords. She forgot she was at work for a moment, and the feeling of that escaping and free moment, she would find with him time and time again.

Before long he was inviting the places that she didn't even know existed within the city. They were sharing lunches and exchanging stories all while laughing at each other and with each other. They often would drive to a location and just remain seated in the car, losing track of time and needing to cancel their original plans. Time flowed by smoothly when they were together. One fair evening while waiting to pick up cheese curds and caramel dip from their local deli, Don reached for Elle's hand and expressed himself unlike he had ever before.

"You know, time is different with you." Elle glanced at him and could feel that what he was saying, was deeper than what was at the surface. She just nodded. "I mean it, it's not regular time, it is literally slower. I can taste each second of it, all while simultaneously gulping it all down." She wanted to reciprocate what he was saying to her but simply did not know how to. "No matter now," he continued, "I want to show you something. Some...where actually." Don grabbed her hand and lead Elle towards his vehicle. She had forgotten all about the cheese curds now, which would later surprise her that evening while recollecting the day's events, due to her utter fascination with cheese and all its variants.

Don drove slightly above the speed limit, while slightly smiling all the while. Elle's interest and anxiety levels were elevated as they drove past the city limit and the radio station began to static in and out. She trusted Don, extremely, so she just grasped his hand a drew in a deep breath. After a little while longer the radio station was completely static. "That's our first clue, my dear, the steady static."

"Clue?" questioned Elle.

"Yes."

"Are there many of these?"

"Four." He kept driving along the road which was no longer a highway, just a paved road along the hilly countryside. They soon began to see tiny Joshua Trees sprouted across the fields that grew in size the more they drove. "This is the beginning of Joshua Hills, Elle."

Perplexed by what she was seeing, Elle rolled down her window to really soak in the scenery. "I thought Joshua trees no longer existed?" asked Elle.

"Not many people know of these parts of the world, and even fewer question what they are taught." Don pointed to his side of the vehicle to show her just how far these trees went on. "Second clue is these Joshua trees we are approaching here. I know it's your first time seeing these, but I'm sure you already can tell how no two trees are alike. Yet look here," Don slowed the vehicle down to just a few miles per hour, "these twenty right here are exactly alike. Size, shape, branches, all of it, to the very number of needles coming out of it. Pluck one out and one will grow in its place soon after." Don placed the car in park as Elle marveled at the sight. Indeed, there were twenty, perfectly alike. Her astonishment was only trumped by her queries. Don recognized Elle's facial mannerisms by now and took the lead before she unloaded her questions. "There is much more here than we can see, you just have to trust me, and go with the flow. Don't get bogged down by needing to know how it all works. Just know that it does."

Don stepped out of the vehicle as Elle remained to marvel at what was right in front of her eyes. Don managed to walk around the vehicle, open the passenger side door, and extend his arm towards Elle all without her ever blinking. She remained fixed in her seat just as much as she was fixated on the Joshua Trees. Her lips began to move a little and it became obvious that she was counting. Counting the trees, the branches, and trying to make sense of it all still. A quick snap from Don's fingers and she had lost her count, frowned her face a bit, and glanced over to his hand. She accepted his invitation and grabbed his hand. As they walked towards the trees, their hands never separated.

"It's called an Anomaly, Elle. These trees are too perfect, not really part of this world, yet still pf it. You see, it's meant to camouflage perfectly well within its surrounding. One would need to know what they are looking for in order to locate this Anomaly. Even then, for it to become activated, it needs to be either Sunrise or Sunset." Elle took a deep breath in, knowing that she had a file cabinet full of questions.

She spoke. "You said, this Anomaly. As in, there are more?" A piece of her wanted these trees to be the only Anomaly around. To think that there were more would just make her feel like her existence was so small. Yet, for there to be more of these, would mean that there was actually much more to this world and life than she had previously known. Regardless of what she has been just exposed to, it fascinated her. "Answer me already," Elle demanded as she tugged his arm.

With a chuckle, he glanced at her at stated simply "Yes." He didn't want to stray too far from the topic at hand, nor did he want to stray too far from focusing on the place they were currently in. "Another time mayhap, stay present with me, stay focused." Elle reconstructed her face to a more serious tone, gave him a short nod, and then began pulling his hand towards the trees.

Don continued to talk as Elle gazed at the Joshua Tress they were pacing towards. "At sunrise or sunset, once the Sun is aligned to the center of the Anomaly, it becomes activated. Once activated, the third and fourth clues become present, and then it is up to the person or people inside of it to complete the process. These final clues that arise during that very specific time frame, are strong enough to disorientate those not meant to travel. If by some slim chance there was a randomer that happened to be in the Anomaly at that very precise time frame, they would leave in doubt and probably fear. It has been recorded by the regular public as eerie places, or spots of mystery, yet they do not know what truly lies there is actually an Anomaly."

"Okay, but you did say travel, right?" Normally there was no need for anyone to repeat what they were saying since she prided herself in being an excellent listener; even when there was an abundance of information being thrown at her. Today it seemed, however, the information that was being thrown at her was not overwhelming necessarily, just out of her scope of knowledge. "I thought the Anomaly was the destination? asked Elle.

"It is, on this planet, yet it is merely a means of transportation to other Anomalies. Anomalies are found all over the vast universe, on every planet, covering every solar system, over multiple dimensions. The true map of the universe is unknown and part of my job is to discover as many as possible. Then there are the much rarer Anomalies to find, which lead to Waypoints. This one in particular leads to the Joshua Hills Waypoint. Waypoints are neither part of any realm, nor are they a world itself. They exist in between all that, independently with their own rules and energy source. Imagine, if you will, a spiderweb. Fully formed and intact. The ends of the web connect different aspects of reality itself, the foundation of creation itself. Then, the web itself is the countless and complex realms that extended into the far reaches of the universe. The spaces in between the webs spun are like the Waypoints I'm talking about, suspended in between all that is tangible, but yet would not exist without the structure it is surrounded by. Valeria, the main location where we study and learn our craft, is also designated as one of these areas that are in-between dimensions"

Elle immediately understood everything he had told just her. There was no doubt in her mind that all this was not only true but important information. It was like everything he was saying before now was teetering between an elaborate joke, or the unrealized truth she had always known to be there. After hearing this last part, she knew there was no way it was a joke, and that her mind could never return to the place it lived before having this information. Don recognized that she had not missed a beat and had been tracking along very well. "I am telling you this because I know you can handle it. I brought you here because I want you to see it for yourself." Don grabbed her other hand and took a step towards her.

There was but half a foot in between them. They stood there for a moment, gazing into each other's eyes in silence. "There is a reason I am drawn to you Elle, and you have always known you were bigger than yourself, bigger than what this city can ever provide for you. You have this innate positive aura about you that I felt instantly the moment we met. Lately, my connection to you has only grown stronger and in the quiet moments that our eyes connect in silence, I can feel your aura pressing upon my soul. And when you smile at me, I feel weightless—" Elle lunged at him while pulling his hands past her waist and around her back, hugging her. Hands still held behind her back, their lips met as they have numerous times before, however, there was something different about this kiss. There was heighten passion, combined with a sense of eternalness, highlighted with a dash of lust.

Emotions raced through Elle's veins infused with passion. Don hesitated to push his lips against hers. The hesitation was only mental, however, for there was not a single break in his body's actual movement. Elle's lips began to part as his eyelids begin to close. Don fought the urge to stare long into the beauty that was. Utter passion was the only thing in existence in the air that surrounded them. Despair for a brief instant, made a known presence, whispering that the moment will eventually end, even though it has not fully commenced. This despair causes Elle's temperature to rise. However, relaxation soon eased in as she realized the heat was actually caused by his body being pressed against hers. A rushing breath of an inhaled gasp fought past her exhale of a low sigh. Don's hands shook with an addicting quiver, that was only steadied by the fix provided by her radiating cheek. Finally, each crevice of her tender lips fit into the impatient grooves of Don's lips, indicating this moment was truer than time. An effortless kiss, perfectly placed. This caused an effect of tingling nerve cells felt on each of their fingertips. The movement of their lips was graceful as the fluid motions of an eagle's wings soaring above open oceans. Their lips briefly parted, but that moment was unbearably long, so they rapidly dove into a new secured position of blissful eternity.

Caresses from his hand ran down along the skin of her spine, just as drops of rain would glide down the petals of roses, feeling the bumps of each vertebra. Even with their eyes closed, they could sense the world spinning, as their bodies started to gravitate even closer together. Slowly like the drift of clouds in the sky, a smile arose from Elle's face as Don once again placed his palm on her cheek. He slid his hand from her cheek, grazing past under her earlobe and grip the back of her neck. He drew her in even closer. The two now kissed heavier and harder. Their tongues wrestling for control that neither had. Elle retreated for an instant to draw breath, and Don followed only her bottom lip. He bit her lip and goosebumps on her neck emerged. He pulled back with lip intact between his teeth, gave it a gentle suckle, and temporarily released it back to her. Her hands went from firmly placed on his hips to pulling and drawing him even closer. Their bodies were compressed and there was no separating them. They were feeling each other not only with their hands but with the rest of their body as well. After kissing and kissing, and kissing, and kissing, a moment of simultaneous breath being drawn in led to a natural pause of their unnatural passion. They gazed into each other's eyes as Don's hands caressed her cheek one final time that evening.

"Lay down with me and let's wait for the Sun to fall," whispered Don. Elle took his hand and began to walk to the nearest Joshua Tree in the Anomaly. She placed her back against the smooth bark and slide down until she was sitting with her legs stretched out in front of her.

"Better yet, come place your head here and relax," she said while patting her lap. Don realized that he was nothing but completely hers at that moment. He was drawn in by her lovingly tone of voice, he could not refuse. He laid on the ground, with his head on her lap and he gazed upon the horizon. She began to tenderly caress his head and play with his hair. There was no more peaceful place on Earth at that moment. No better place to be. A blissful tear emerged from the corner of his eye, and as he fought to draw it back in. Then a warm tear fell on his temple. He glanced up and saw that Elle too was overcome with emotion and the tear belonged to her. Elle gazed into the distance and allowed all the warm orange colors blended against the green of the trees to influence her. She too was in immense peace; unlike she has ever felt before. She glanced down and looked at Don's protruding tear that would not fall, and wiped it away for him.

No words needed to be spoken. No words could be spoken.

CHAPTER 4

D on began to drift away into a slumber as Elle continued to stoke his hair. The wind around them began to fade away as well. The bottom crest of the Sun began to touch the horizon and this is what alerted Don back into a fully awaken state. He sat up and placed his body parallel to the Sun. "Come here" he said as he patted the ground in front of him.

"Is it time?" asked Elle as she scooted inch by inch until she too was parallel to the sun, but sitting with her back against the sun, and sitting directly in front of him. He nodded his head in affirmation, and took both her hands into his. He knew there were only minutes left until half the Sun reached the horizon and the Anomaly fully activated, yet he could not resist from gazing into Elle's eyes in silence. Elle felt his gaze peer into her, and Don felt her gaze peer into his. For a brief moment in this wondrous place, two souls recognized each other from centuries past, and a harmonic peace was instilled deep inside of them. They drew in a deep breath simultaneously and the moment had dissipated.

"The final two clues are more felt then seen." Don began. "What you will first feel is a sort of inner vibration. Imagine a large tuning fork being stuck and placed right next to your ear. You will hear that vibration get louder and louder

17

and you will feel the vibration build in your chest until it consumes you. Lastly you will feel extremely heavy. Your body and mind will slow down and you will feel as if gravity itself was an old friend who has now welcomed you back into the ground."

"This is why we are sitting." Elle remarked, more as a statement rather than a question. Don warmly smiled, and she smiled back.

"Both the vibrations and the weight of your own body will increase until they take over all your senses, and this will now be the only thing you know." Don glanced over at the Sun and his experienced body already started to feel the effects press in. "Take deep breathes and let go of your mind. Keep taking these deep breathes and concern yourself with nothing, Have no fear. Have no joy. Be nothing and let yourself become something that is not anything. Expect nothing, but prepare for anything. Then simply let go, and trust that you will find me on the other side."

The center of the Sun was now perfectly aligned with the Anomaly.

CHAPTER 5

The sun flashed like a photo was being taken. The light took over Elle's field of vision. Her eyes shut due to the brightness, yet the light remained. She began to see small spots and orbs of light floating behind her eyelids. Gradually they all faded and the darkness began to take over as it should have with closed eyelids, yet full darkness never really took over. Elle would see shapes here and there, appear and disappear. These random shapes were filled with static electricity looking white dots and blurs. Flashes of white light would jolt into view. Then, off to the distance there were small white orbs of light. This light grew closer and larger. At first, the depth perception did not make sense, because her eyes were closed, but she immediately dismissed that motion. She knew she had to be clear-minded as possible.

The orbs grew in size and a faint hum began to ring in her ears. She was too focused on the orbs of light to notice the steadily growing hum. When the steady hum turned into a broken-up vibrating tune, she realized that her body had been growing tired and heavy. This was all happening too fast and too simultaneous that she could not keep track of all the changes. She supposed this would prevent her from being overly fixated with only one of the sensations. Her field of view was now completely immersed in light and she heard the vibrating hum coming out of her head rather than it entering her ears. Her chest felt like it was sinking into the ground and that the rest of her limbs were following close behind. As she melted into the ground with her chest leaning forward and vibrating, her eyes spotted a darker circle appear in front of her. She wanted to turn away but had no head to do so. She was just a vibrating blob on the ground it felt like. The void of the dark circle grew larger in size but the larger it grew, the more colors appeared to be emanating from it. Every time the sounds of the vibrations grew a decibel louder, a thump was felt in her chest and another color emerged from the void.

"Take a deep breath!" she heard Don say as the words echoed through her brain. She did not know if she was just recollecting that sound, or if he was actually there, somewhere behind the tunnel of colors and thick vibrations that now shook her entire essence. As she drew in a deep breath, the tunnel of colors began to race towards her and suddenly she was engulfed in it and racing through it. The tunnel turned left and right, curved down and back up, and seemed to never have an end. The vibrations were now picking up in tempo until they were once again a steady hum but with the added loudness like a jet engine that was hovering above her, instead of flying over. It was all too much to bear. She had to take another breath in. Her heavy body then began to free-fall straight into the tunnel of marvelous colors and lights. Then, at last, the vibrating hum grew so loud and intense, that it decimated her melting body into an oblivion of atoms, which no longer made up a human named Elle. Rather the only thing that existed now was an Elle that was like no other.

She felt that she was then rapidly slingshot into a brief wave of darkness and light that strobed in front of her. A single shock wave of numbing vibrations jolted from her heart outwards towards her limbs and she felt it go past the outside of her body. Grey matter washed over her and turned everything dark behind her eyelids, which she once again had. All she saw was a greyish matter fade to black. Her eyes could have been lifted now, but she still felt slightly heavy. Her body tingled as she began to squeeze her hands into fists, and then open them again stretching each finger outwards.

Elle took a deep breath again. This time, after she exhaled, her eyelids lifted. It was at this moment that she has wished she asked Don what exactly she was expecting to see, but he was always mysterious like that. She knew that he liked her to experience things for herself, for her to make up her own mind about things without his external input. Yet, this time, she for sure wished she knew what to expect, if only, just to verify that she was at the right place.

The first thing she noticed was that there were Joshua Trees in the area, not nearly as many as there were just mere moments ago, but still very much around. Next, and very obvious were the dozens of doors that were now in her field of view. All the same standard wooden structure with a doorknob. They were certainly not all facing the same direction, nor did they appear to be in any particular order. Nothing too unique about them except for the fact that they were all closed and seemed to be randomly assorted in the field. She pondered momentarily the amount of work that needed to take place in order for all of them to be installed the way they were. They were clearly a permanent fixture in the ground that had to be dug beneath them in order for them not to fall over. It was probably the only thing that astonished her more than the fields of doors. The sheer number of holes that had to be dug in order to install all of those doors had to take nothing short of decades. She would soon find out that these doors were always a part of the ground, just as the grass and trees were.

Elle had a mind that worked in that sort of way. Every time she was fascinated by something, not too soon after, she would contemplate the mechanics, logistics, and steps needed to be taken in order for said fascination to occur. Her next obvious thought centralized on the purpose of the doors being so scattered. It would seem that it would be much easier to keep track of them if they were just in rows and columns. There was a chaotic beauty to what she was viewing however, the doors and trees all co-existing in a mostly barren land. Behind the field that was immediately in front of her, were hills that seemed to be as barren as the ground she was now on. Upon the hills, there too appeared to be numerous doors.

"Don?" Elle began to look around in search of her partner in crime. She scanned along the field and up the hills. She even fixated at certain doors as if he might have been hiding behind one. She looked behind the trees and again by the hills. Nothing was seen but these damn doors and few Joshua Trees. She has been standing still long enough for her to feel the heels of her feet begin to tingle, any longer and they certainly would have gone numb. She took her first steps in this strange field of doors and continued to search for Don. She grew upset before becoming worried about him. She knew that he would be able to take care of himself, she knew that this was his idea and was not as lost as she was. What she could not figure out, was the reason that his presence was not there in a moment where she could really have used it. She took a deep breath in and realized there has to be a reason, and then continued to pace forward; not knowing if that was the right direction, or even if a place like this had directions. That deep breath she took came accompanied by a musty odor of damp wood. Which made sense with all the wooden doors around, yet the floor was not wet, nor were the doors.

This odor remained persistent as she walked past a few standing doors.

She was inclined to grab a doorknob and see if it even operated as a regular doorway, or if they were more like an art statement being presented at an installation. She began to walk towards the one nearest her and reached out her right hand. As her hand neared the brass doorknob, that same vibrating hum that she heard back at the Anomaly Point, began to ring in her ears. She drew her hand immediately back, but not completely. Of course, she needed to ensure that her previous action was the source of this noise. She reached once again towards the doorknob and again the hum became audible. With this confirmation, Elle decided that she should continue with her first instinct, which was to find Don. She scanned the area again for any new information. Her search yielded no new results, so she continued down the same direction she was set on before. Passing door after door she remained tempted to reach out and experiment again, but with every door that passed, she grew more curious as in where Don had been.

By the time she was halfway up the first steep hill, she realized how quickly she had grown accustomed to the damp wood odor in the air. She took a moment to pause her climb as she began to feel the lactic acid building up in her quadriceps. Elle began to grow worried that perhaps something went wrong at the Anomaly, that perhaps she did something wrong and was going to be stuck here. She drew in a deep breath to calm her nerves, and just past the smell of damp wood, she detected something else. This time she took a more purposeful breath, a more hopeful one. The odor that came to her was that of chestnuts being roasted. A smell she did not know she was so familiar with until that very moment. It had been years since she smelled a chestnut being roasted, even longer since she ate one. Here she was now, tired of standing and hungry for chestnuts.

With a new sense of excitement, Elle began to lunge up the last bit of steep hill that was left. By the time she reached the top, she was almost fully crawling up the grainy dirt and had gotten a chunk of it in her nose and mouth. She wiped it away with her forearm but left a trail of it on her cheek. As her arm returned to her waist, she could now see a two-story cottage built from stone, with smoke coming out of the chimney not too far off in the distance. She felt relief knowing that Don would be there, and there was no question about his presence not being there. She felt him there.

Approaching the cobbled steps that lead to the center door, Elle was uncertain of the amount of time she wanted to stay, primarily due to the fact that she did not understand this place much. The only thing she was certain about was that she wanted some of those chestnuts. She turned the knob, with no vibrational hum noted, and swung the door open.

CHAPTER 6

The door with minimal hinge structure effortlessly glided straight into the wall with a pronounced bang. There, sat Don, at a circular table in the center of the room. There, he sat with two other strangers, one male, one female, never before seen by Elle. There he was, simply just there, instead of being in those fields searching for her. She never wanted to throw something at him so bad as she did right then. He was staring at her with a smug smile on his face. He was proud of her and she could feel that. She never wanted to hug him so bad as she did right then.

Don threw his hands up in the air and he rose from his seat and shouted "There she is!" He casually walked over to her and wrapped his arms around her and squeezed. Tension fell from Elle's shoulders as she intensely hugged back. He wiped the trail of dirt from her cheek and kissed the area softly.

"We were wondering just how long it would take you." said the man seated at the table. "We thought maybe the robot bears ate you!" The man then stood up and began to walk towards her in a mechanical manner, hands in the air with fingers spread out all while continuously growling.

"Chris, stop it. That's how you wanna introduce

yourself?" Said Dayna, the lady seated next to him. Chris then paused his movement and staggered over to Dayna while never breaking the robot-bear character. He hunched over her, grabbed her arm, and began fake chomping at it. Dayna began to giggle and slap his back a few times. "Seriously, seriously, okay babe, don't be rude to our new guest." Chris playfully wrestled with her arm a little longer and let go with one final growl.

Don placed his arm on Elle's lower back and gently nudged her toward the table. "Meet Chris, who is completely joking about robot-bears being out there, and Dayna his wife. They own this abode and have been gracious hosts to me for the last few years." Don pulled out a chair for her to sit in and walked over to Chris, He began playfully stabbing at his ribcage. "Where is that off switch you robot-bear, I'll find it I tell ya!" The two began to wrestle with each other as Elle just stared in confusion, but with slight amusement.

As the two continued to stab each other's ribs with their fingertips portraying imaginary blades, Dayna placed her hand on Elle's forearm and asked "Can I get you something to drink, hon?"

"Water would be great," Elle said. Dayna stood up and walked over to the kitchen which was still visible from where the table was located. The panting from Chris and Don signaled that their roughhousing was almost over. Its termination was eagerly anticipated by Elle, due to the numerous questions that were now occupying all her thinking power. A moment later Chris and Don gave each other a quick tap hug and returned to the table.

Chris looked over to her, "We would have some snacks ready for you but we had no idea when you would arrive, Elle" Chris reorganized his shirt and placed a more serious face on. "How did you manage, your first travel and all?"

"It's nice to meet the both of you," said Elle loud enough for Dayna to hear also, "but Don and I left at the same time, what do you mean you had no clue when I would arrive?" Elle realized that her tone may have been too straightforward, but did not know how to recover from it. Chris glanced over to Don and punched him in the shoulder.

"This poor girl, what's wrong with you man? Did you forget to brief her?" Chris asked

"I told her what I had too, the rest was for her to figure out. I knew she could handle it." Don turned his face and now spoke to Elle, "I knew you could handle it."

"Okay, but where were you?" Elle asked as Dayna walked back towards her and placed a glass of water on the coaster by her hands.

"So, time works a little different out here, hon," said Dayna. "Don waited for you a few hours before he came here. He told us he wanted to bring you over a few months ago, and by the way he speaks of you, we couldn't wait to meet you either."

"So how many hours has it been?" asked Elle

Chris couldn't help but chuckle a little, "It's umm, been, well a couple of days to be honest."

"Days? What?" Elle sunk her head into her shoulders as her eyebrows raised. "How could it have been days if we left at the same time?" Elle realized her mouth was open for longer than she was comfortable with and reached for her glass to drink.

Don began, "My body, mind, and spirit are more accustomed to traveling in that sort of way. The travel between Anomalies doesn't always take a specific amount of time. The variables involved in the length of travel are multifaceted. Experience with said Anomaly, amount of focus during travel, amount of fear, how relaxed you are, how much you can let go, I don't know, it's just so many things that go into it." Don went from sounding like a professional to a clueless toddler, yet somehow it made sense for Elle.

"For the past two days, Don went looking four times a day for you through those fields and hills," Dayna said proudly. "But we are certainly glad you made it to us. You must have felt him. Your body and mind did the rest." Elle began to overanalyze how exactly it was that she took the path that she did. She could not really place them in chronological order. Don interrupted her train of thought by thumping her thigh with his thigh under the table.

"It's okay. As I said, just let go, and I knew you could handle it." Don reassured with a wink.

"You're also lucky the storms have been away the past few weeks. It would have sucked to pop in during the middle of these storms we've been having. I swear they are becoming more frequent." Chris said.

"Rain doesn't really bother me," said Elle.

"These aren't storms of rain, hon." Dayna chimed in. "They're electrical storms that produce lightning bolts, yes, but mostly they just knock out all of our electrical systems for a time being. They come abruptly and it's difficult to prepare for them. The longest we went without power was about seven weeks." Elle took a look around the Abode and realized that most of the light in the room was naturally occurring, and compared to her apartment back on Earth, there were not too many electrical products in use. "Depending on what project Chris is working on for Valeria, if the power is out for too long, we usually just leave the Waypoint and settle up some-realm else. These storms are one of the reasons that Chris and I have started to look for somewhere else to—"

DING!

"Chestnuuuuuts!" Don jumped from his chair at the sound of the oven, and began growling, and started mechanically lunging towards the oven. "Robot Bear wants more. Chestnuts now. Roawrr!" Don reached the oven and opened it. "I've been craving these for a while now. No one makes chestnuts like Dayna. The only other thing that can compete is her 10 Cheese Mac-N-Cheese with bacon and scallions." He brought a bowl over to the table, along with a side of Dayna's homemade apple vanilla sauce. The four began to snack on the chestnuts and Don smiled from ear to ear the entire time.

"Now that you are home, Elle, the night can officially begin." Chris slammed his fist on the table and shouted "Here, here! Babe, bring the moonshine!" The way Chris said, "you are home," stuck out to Elle, and it warmed her heart. It sounded so casually perfect.

Drinks were poured, laughs were had, questions were asked, and the night progressed with a barrage of snacks continuously revolving from the kitchen to the table. Never was there an empty glass or mouth without crumbs. They played games and listened to music. Chris and Dayna told stories that would bring Elle to tears of laughter, mostly at Don's expense, which seemed to be completely fine with him. Elle has never seen Don so animated and in his own skin with other people. It not only amused her but made her feel comfortable being there as well. In such little time, Elle had found comfort in them, just the way Don has in his years of being there.   Throughout the night Don would move about the entire room but always find time to sit right next to Elle and caressed her hand, at least for a moment or two. He tendered to her and ensured that not a beat of uncomfortably stirred within her. Nearing the end of the night Don left to use the bathroom and Dayna took this opportunity to sit next to Elle.

"No, but seriously hon, you two aren't dating?" asked Dayna

"Oh, let her be," said Chris

"You. Shoo." Dayna sucked her teeth. "Go, uncork another bottle and leave us to our girl talk." Chris raised his hands in submission and walked over to the kitchen. "You two look so natural together. And the way you look at each other in passing, well let's say I know that look." Elle smiled and glanced down at her almost empty glass. She began to tap the side of it with her fingernail.

"You aren't the first one to mention this." Elle continued to tap her glass. "Of course, I love him, but we are not in love. Does that make sense? There is too much in his mind. I feel it during random moments when we talk for hours. He is consumed. I doubt there is any room for a real relationship in there." Elle looked up at Dayna now. "Plus, I'm not ready either." Don walked into the room, saw the two sitting on the couch, glanced over at Chris fumbling with a new bottle of Moonshine and began to tiptoe towards him.

"I know, hon. I know the feeling. You'll see that time isn't the only thing that works differently here. A lot of things do. Chris and I have been here for a long time. Longer than most who travel through here. We are from different planets, both human-occupied, yes, but from different solar systems. I used to think it was by chance that we met here, but now, I am certain that chance was only a small factor in this. We came here to help map the unknown universe, but we stayed to help navigate our hearts. Eventually, our time will come to move on from this Waypoint, but when we do it will be to another world, a simple one, unlike the Earth you two come from." Elle was gripped by their story, wanted to know more, wanted to stay up the rest of the night talking to her and ask her everything.

Dayna took a pause and glanced over to the boys. "Robot Bear!" she shouted and alerted Chris. He turned his head to query the outburst, and Don was forced to pounce on his back. The two then wrestled on the ground while growling and attempting to make machine and robot noises. Dayna and Elle both laughed and resumed their conversation. "What you and Don have is certainly special. Although it may end tomorrow, years from now, or never at all, just know that he brought you here in order to share a very special piece of himself with you. He cares for you truly." Dayna embraced Elle and a true friendship was forged.

"I know he does, and thank you," Elle said as she squeezed Dayna into her arms. This evening was not what she was expecting, but it was what she unknowingly needed. Elle looked at the boys wrestling around on the floor and couldn't help but admire the jovial masculinity of the two. "Guys, c'mon, our glasses are empty," she said while swirling her empty glass in the air. The two scraping men paused for a moment, measuring each other out for any surprise attacks as they both raised to their feet. A short laugh and another tap hug, and the two were now baristas in the kitchen pouring drinks.

Chris walked over first and handed over a fresh glass to Dayna. "Listen here you two love-nerds," said Chris.

"It's birds!" shouted Don from the kitchen.

"Right, whatever, same-same," Chris said as she gestured with his hand flat in front of him by flipping it over and back. "The Lil lady and I here are going for a walk. A nightly stroll around the area to see the doors crawl." Chris reached out for Dayna's hand while giving her a slow wink. Dayna smiled and sent him a wink as well. "You two settle in and we will see ya when we see ya."

"Cheers buddy, see you soon," said Don walking back into the room. Chris and Dayna walked out the front door. Don with two glasses in hand began walking up the steps that lead to the upper level, and Elle was right behind him.

CHAPTER 7

As Don went up the steps his mind was racing over whether or not his living quarters were a mess. He did not think that Elle would judge him, yet he did not want to appear completely unkempt. He hastened his pace to arrive with at least some time in front of Elle just in case. His living quarters were not originally designed to house a person. It was simply an area next to the only balcony of the abode. After living on the couch for six months and creating a bond with Chris and Dayna, the two surprised him with a setup that Don was thrilled to have. There was no door to the room, so as Don reached those final steps, he quickly scanned the area as was pleased to realize that it was not in bad shape. His bed which was made from some sort of gel material from Chris's home planet was tucked away against the far wall. A dresser, a small desk, and a chair with a communication TeleQuick station were on the near wall. Everything else in the room was scrapes and artifacts from the various worlds he already traveled to from this Waypoint. The tall doors of the balcony were partially opened and were letting a subtle wind in that carried that musty wooden odor.

"Home, sweet home," Don said as he raised his arms, drinks still in hand, and performed an about-face. Elle smiled and clapped with only two fingers from each hand. "Oh, does the arena not please the crowd?" asked Don.

Elle asked, "Where's all the colorful artwork I know you so fond of?"

"You're stepping on it actually." Don gestured to the floor and Elle immediately took a step back. All she saw was a wooden floor and a small area rug near the bed. Don began to give a hearty laugh and Elle realized he had just been joking. "It is on my to-do list, for sure. Mayhap, you can also bring one for me from your place next time." Elle took a few steps forward and took a look around. She was intrigued with his setup of practicality, but with a sense of home also. She could tell that he had lived there for quite some time. "Come to the balcony, I want to show you something." Don swung open both doors and placed the drinks on the ledge of the balcony. She slowly walked over to him as she took the scenery in. The wooden musty odor was not pleasant the first time she was introduced to it, but up here it was far less appalling. Slightly fitting she thought as she placed her hands on the ledge. Although the abode was no more than two stories high, its position on the land had an astonishing view.

The night sky was filled with stars of all sizes. It lit up the fields of doors and created an illusion as if they were floating along the sea. She noticed there was no Moon, however, there were two robust planets that were filling the view of the sky. The two neighboring planets seem to glow and radiate. All the light was coming directly from them. Elle noticed for the first time that one of the planets actually had a tiny moon near it, difficult to see but certainly there. She was fixated on it. "Are there...others, on those Planets?" she asked.

"Mayhap"

"You have no clue?" Elle asked softly, as she was still locked on the tiny moon.

"Chris thinks he has met people from there but he was not sure. In my time here I have asked the same question to those that I encounter. Shrugs is what I mostly get."

"When I approached a door earlier, I felt and heard the same vibration I felt while going through the Anomaly."

Don nodded his head. "Yeaup, going through the doors from this Waypoint is very similar as going through the Anomaly. There are some differences though. Mainly, what you should know is that nothing would have happened if you did open the door, you would simply just see the other side of the field it was on. You need an activated Wrist-Vector." Don reached into his pocket and displayed a chrome band with a pyramid shapes centerpiece made out of a crystal of sorts. He slipped it onto his wrist and flicked his wrist outward. The crystal pyramid emanated a blue light and then began to dim slowly until it no longer glowed. Don took it off and handed it to Elle.

"How did you get it to glow?" Elle asked as she began her thorough inspection.

"It synchronizes with its owner, and will only work for them. It takes anywhere from one to two years to construct one. It uses a precise build formula that involves numerous rare materials. Chris helped me make this one." Elle slipped it on and bounced her arm as if weighing it. "Not only do you need it to go through the doors, but it tells you when it's time to come back. The thing about this Waypoint is that the doors move every night. We call it crawling. The only way to keep track of the doors already traveled through is by marking it somehow. I usually use a small nick from my blade near the doorknob. When the doors crawl into different positions in the land, the connection to the door becomes deactivated. Then, the only way to return is by having someone come get you with a new Wrist-Vector."

"So, you're just stuck there?" Elle had a more inquisitive look than a worried one.

"Just as time works differently here compared to Earth, each realm has its own time structure as well. Dayna lost Chris for 3 years once. Not three years of Joshua Hills time, but in whatever realm Chris was in. It took Dayna only a few months to build a new Wrist-Vector, but Chris was stuck living a different life for about three years. If they didn't already have a stash of most of the components and raw material needed, it could've taken Dayna much longer to build one, leaving Chris to live out a decade or two somewhere else. She still had to go Realm-Hopping in order to collect some of the rarer components and raw materials. Here was the tricky part though... not only did she have to build a new Wrist-Vector, she had to keep track of where the door was in order to not lose him for good. Each and every night she would have to go out to the fields and watch where the door crawled to." Elle let out a heavy sigh. Her inquisitive face morphed to one of worry momentarily, but then returned back as she continued to fiddle with Don's Wrist-Vector.

"Can it break?" asked Elle.

"It can. It's difficult to damage one to the point of non-functionality, but it's possible. There are also a lot more functions that these things can do, but I'll tell you at a later time."

"I want one!" Elle laughed as she tossed it back to Don.

"Actually, it's why I brought you here, I want you to talk to Chris so we can start making you one. He needs some of your DNA. Blood or Saliva work best."

"Wait, what?" Elle was now squarely facing him. "I was just joking."

"There's still so much more I want to show you.

Through these doors are worlds and places unlike you have ever seen. I want you to see what is out there, I want you to join me." Elle's already large eyes seemed to grow even more. She opened her mouth to speak but Don cut her off. "Not join me as in let's get married and explore like Chris and Dayna, but be at my side for a little, maybe even join the team if you decide you want a change of pace."

"I thought you had to go through vigorous training to become a Realm Seeker?" questioned Elle.

"Eventually you would have to go through the course but until then there are other methods. Unorthodox sure, but not unheard of, and I think you're a natural. It only took you two days to go through your first Anomaly trip. Average is five at best, sometimes an entire week even."

The ground rumbled for a brief moment. The glasses fell from the ledge and landed on the cobblestone below. The ground rumbled again. Don reached for Elle's hand and pulled her in close. "Look, the doors are about to crawl." The ground was surely still rumbling since they could hear it, but they no longer felt it under their feet. Tiny pebbles on the ground began to dance and hop on the floor. The few Joshua Trees around shook a tiny bit, causing dry needles to fall. Then all the doors began to move inch by inch in all directions. Although each door moved without changing direction, they all seemed to be crawling along purposefully in order to not run into each other. Never has Don heard anyone speak of two doors colliding. This sort of organized chaos was marvelous to witness. The way the fields and the hills looked under the night sky made it appear like it was a show production intended for the residents of Joshua Hills.

Elle reached out her hand, requesting to see the Wrist-Vector again. She slipped in on and admired it "Do you think I'd look good with one of my own?" Don took a step towards her and placed his hands on her hip.

"You already know I think you look beyond good, all the time." The crawling of the doors began to slow down as they shuffled into their new residence for the new day. They crept slowly through the ground, dragging the dirt alongside them. The rumble on the ground increased again indicating the final settlement of the doors. The ground-shaking caused Elle's loose shirt to slip down a reveal the skin of her shoulder. Don looked into her eyes, his pupil dilated, his breath became shallow. Elle picked up on all these subtleties and reach for the other side of her shirt and pulled it down revealing both shoulders. Don leaned forward and kiss her now revealed collar bone. As he drew back, he slowly blew on the moist spot. She grabbed him by the back of his neck and guided it back deep into her neck. Don began kissing her again as she used her free hand to slide down his arm and onto the button of his shorts, where she eagerly unbuttoned it. Don took another step forward, but with nowhere to go they tumbled and fell onto the balcony floor. Their kisses grew into groans, and their groans into heavy breathing. With the light from the two planets reflecting off their naked bodies, their first sexual encounter occurred, and they remained there until they both fell asleep staring into the starry night.

CHAPTER 8

Don was the first to awaken from his slumber. It was still night. Not more than a few hours passed, but that was all he was really accustomed to sleeping lately. He stood up, walked to his dresser, and tossed on the first pair of shorts and tank top he could find. After all, is time there, he has yet to own any pants. The climate of Joshua Hills Waypoint resembled the summer nights from back on Earth. He wasn't sure if Elle would want to place her same clothes back on, so he began looking in his drawers for something loose and comfortable for her. As he hunched over to open the last drawer, he felt someone touch his back.

"Did you forget that you're not the only one who doesn't sleep much," Elle stated rhetorically. Don rose to meet Elle's gaze, but could not resist looking up and down at her still naked body. He reluctantly handed over the clothes he grabbed for her since he just wanted to go and lie with her again. He wanted to feel her body next to his, pressed upon each other and allowing for their body heat to unite them. As she dressed, he noticed that he was admiring her like a painting at a museum, examining and admiring all of her curves, skin tones, and unique birthmarks. He always recalled her beauty in his mind, but her presence there, in his actual home, placed her in a different type of light. He was excellent at separating work from his personal life, yet at this moment he did not know which was which. He was unsure if having someone from Earth enter his Waypoint home would emotionally interrupt his focus. He was sure, however, that Elle had a natural talent to free her mind, and that there was certainly a connection between them. This was something that he could not, and would not ignore. Having sex with Elle did not make him yearn for her anymore he noticed. He realized at that moment that he had already yearned for her, much before that moment, and much deeper than sex could have changed things. He also realized that what he felt was something unlike he had before, it felt ancient and ever-present. She was not only a friend, but a partner in his journey through life, the ones before and perhaps the lives he has yet to live.

Elle finished getting dressed and hugged him. She sank into him and Don knew that they would not be moving for a bit. "Now what?" she asked.

"Now nothing you already don't know." He took a few paces left so he could lean against the wall, making sure to keep his arms constantly around Elle, as to not disrupt her comfortability. "Only a few moments have passed back on Earth since you reached us in the afternoon. Chris and I will work on your Wrist-Vectorand then when you are ready, I'll show you around and you can then decide what you want to do." Don knew the adventures that laid ahead were temporary, as temporary as anything in the known universe he supposed. However, he would do his best to create an impermeable bubble around them. A notional bubble that would safeguard them from becoming too attached to one another in order to preserve the good as long as possible. A part of him knew he could never give up his personal journey and get too involved with Elle. Yet, another part of him knew nothing at all. To get too attached to someone would place them in too much danger. The danger that could arrive at any moment from any one of the unknown worlds that lay beyond those doors. He also knew that he could be called upon for a mission that would take him far away for unknown periods of time. He knew he could not get too attached. He also knew that he was a connoisseur of little knowledge and would remain open to all possibilities.

He smiled at her, "Look, what we have between us will always remain special. No matter where we go or what happens down the road. These times together will be untouched and unscathed by negativity." Don then placed both his hands on her cheeks and guided her face so their eyes could meet. "I love you, there is no denying that, and I know you feel the same. Let us just give these moments in space and time their due attention, for when they are gone, they will remain dear to my heart, as you always will too." Elle placed her hand on his cheeks now.

"I love you," she said and kissed him. Their lips remained compressed on each other's, with no movement to them. Just passionately held there, as the world around them too remained suspended. Elle opened her eyes and look out to the balcony. "Our time together can be like a bubble?" She said with a childlike tone to it. "A bubble not effected by any silly rules. Just us enjoying what life has to offer."

"You're in my head somehow, again. I was thinking the same thing." Don rubbed her cheek with his thumb and chuckled. "You ready to head back?"

"I never knew I could leave Earth, and now you're asking me if I want to return?" Elle spun out of Don's hands and skipped a short way to the balcony. She looked out into the horizon. "I think I'll stay the night."

"Careful now, you may not want to ever leave." Don teased whimsically.

"I still don't know what it is that you really do. How would I ever become a Realm Seeker if I don't know what it is that you do?" He walked over to her and stared into the fields as well.

"We try to find other realms that have intelligent life. Worlds that are also capable of freeing their own minds in order to get to Valeria. We unite organisms from all over the various discovered universes, in order to try and map it. We trade knowledge and resources all while focusing on our main goal which is... the ever-ongoing attempt to improve the living experience at all consciousness levels." Don stated verbatim the text from the introduction manual he received at Valeria. Turns out, however, since being on his own, he learned that there were many more complexities to that statement. But it made sense to him then when he first learned it and hoped it made sense to her now.

"What fortune cookie did you get that from?" Elle said and poked his chest. They shared a laugh, and Don felt that there was nothing else to say at the moment. "It's all truly fascinating, for real. But I don't think I could do this for the rest of my life. It would drive me crazy."

"Who says I'm not?" whiplashed Don.

"I didn't..."

"I know, it just that... I do feel crazy sometimes."

"Don't we all, from time to time?"

"I guess you're right. I mean that's the point of all this anyway. You do it for as long as you can. Some retire old and content, some find a life partner and change course, while others become dismayed and lose hope in themselves. I just don't ever want to be like those last ones, I don't want to lose hope."

"Don, I know you could never, even if you were forced to." Elle hugged him and pulled him down onto the floor. "Come, lay." She patted her thigh and signaled for his head to be placed there. Don obliged. She began to stroke his head and play with his hair as she knew he very much enjoyed it. "Get some rest, I think I'll stay up a litter longer."

CHAPTER 9

"**L**et's go love-nerds!" Shouted Chris from downstairs. The morning sun had risen before either Don or Elle awoke. They woke up on the bed, and it took a moment for him to recall the hasty midnight shuffle from balcony to bed.

They were cuddled up still as Elle returned a shout, "Birds! Dammit Chris it's Birds!"

"Ah, so you agree then!" Chris said. Elle laughed through her nose and rolled out of bed. She began to remove the clothes he had given her the night prior and began redressing herself. Don remained in bed and began to stretch.

"You gonna stick around for breakfast?" he asked.

"Are you going to ask me to stay?"

Don shook his head, "You know I will not. If you wanna stay, by all means then."

"It would be rude if I didn't," Elle said.

"Then you have your answer, babe." Don did want her to stay, yet he was too proud to ask. He told himself that he would never beg anybody to stay. Mostly due to his abandonment issues from being left by his parents as a child, and partially due to pride. He knew it probably was not the smartest thing to commit to, but he felt like he was honest enough with people, that he could secure some of his pride at least. Little did he know that this would later come to slap him in his face, literally.

Don finished his stretches and placed his feet on the floor. He began to take a step forward, but he still had one foot tangled in the sheets unbeknownst to him. He fell forwards and barely caught himself before squishing his nose into the floor. His elbows slammed into the ground below, and Elle's laughter jolted into the sky above. "Are you kidding me?" laughed Elle straight from the belly. She healed over and laughed louder, this time while gasping for some air. "No way that was an accident!" With elbows still on the ground and face now resting on the floor, Don also began to laugh hard.

"That was all planned from the moment you woke up!" lied Don. Don rolled onto his back and watched Elle continue to laugh.

"You wish!" She could barely get the next sentence out. "What was all that stretching for if you were just going to trip the moment you got up?" A few tears gathered in one eye as another began to roll down her cheek from the other eye. Don laughed and began to clap his hands slowly.

"I'm glad you are amused. Now come over and help me up." He said and raised an arm into the air. Elle still hunched over with one hand on her belly, reach over with her free hand. The moment her hands met his, Don yanked her off balance and she tumbled onto the ground beside him.

"You are still laughing," he stated. This was no question; it was more astonishment than anything. They were now both audibly laughing in each other's arms, except Don's arms were throbbing just a bit. He began catching his breath as started to untangle himself. Elle reached over and help him as she too began to regain her normal breath tempo. "Now I'm for sure hungry, let's go."

"I agree, but just...just be careful now" Elle teased

with a satisfied grin on her face. Don rolled his eyes and flashed her a half-smile. The two went down the steps and were met with eager eyes at the table. Chris and Dayna had begun eating already but paused to witness the two come down the steps.

"Well, well." Dayna took a deep breath in, "well, well, what do we have here?"

"A real pair of love-nerds I tell ya," said Chris as he returned to shoveling food back into his mouth. Two plates were already set up for them.

"Thank you, guys, seriously. I feel so welcomed here," said Elle as she placed a napkin on her lap.

"That's because you are you come back anytime." Dayna smiled and then turned to Chris. "Babe, why don't you tell Elle all about how hard you've been working on her Wrist-Vector." Chris stopped chewing and without lifting his head, he nervously raised his eyes slowly to glance over at Don.

"It's okay, I told her already," Don said. With immediate relief, Chris continued to chew his food. "She knows we have been working on it, and she knows the decision is hers if she wants to come back."

"Okay, A, I'm right here; and B, Hell yeah!" Elle folded her hands in front of her plate and batted her eyelashes. "Tell me." Chris rushed the last few spoonsful of food into his mouth and sipped his drink. He leaned over to Dayna and kissed her on the cheek.

"Delicious babe, as always." With a sweet smile on her face, Dayna winked at Chris. "Alright, Elle. Dayna and I know the importance of having a backup Wrist-Vector, however, we can't just make a bunch and have them on standby. The last part of synching a Wrist-Vector to its user has to be done within a certain amount of time. So, we collect what material we can and start the process up to the point of DNA collection. Once that is obtained, then we can continue onto the last few steps." Elle extended her arm with her veins facing up.

"Take what you need coach, I'm ready," Elle said. A quick laugh from the table and Elle returned her arms. She grabbed her fork and began eating her meal. Don, almost complete with his meal reached over and placed his hand on her lap. He caressed it for a moment and excused himself from the table. He walked around and picked up what empty plates remained. While performing a balancing act with the plates, he looked at Chris and signaled him to follow him.

Both Don and Chris began washing the plates while the girls remained at the table. "Thanks for doing this for me," said Don. He reached over and gave Chris a one-armed hug. Chris winked and nodded.

"Listen, Dayna and I aren't going to be hanging around much longer. You know this, but this time I think we are finally ready to move on. This abode is going to be yours, as are all the components and raw materials collected through the years. I don't want to hear shit about it. You are family, and there is no one else that deserves to be here more than you. But, it's time to get serious about this Wrist-Vector building. You have to learn this stuff before we go." Chris paused and faced Don.

"Yeah, I get it. For sure, but it's not like we aren't going to be seeing each other anymore. Like you just stated, we are family." said Don.

"Listen, brother, it's a little more complicated than that." Don, stopped washing the plate and faced him square on. "We are going to a faster world, D."

"What? Where? Have we been there before? When did you decide this?" Don did not want to ask the next question. Don had to ask the next question. "Chris" Don felt heavy.

"How fast?"

"Dayna and I have been there a few times already. It's called Nexus. There's a beach and those sweet frost-berries we both like. It's not just that, it's safe there. Plus, the government does not get too involved with Valeria. You already know that after I was lost for a few years, Dayna caused quite a bit of commotion to get some of the raw material quicker. Since then, it hasn't been the same."

"Fuck that!" Don shouted. The girls stopped their chatter and glance over. Elle was shocked, but Dayna was not. Dayna stood up and walked over to her. She said something inaudible to Don and the two girls walked outside. "I can fix that; you know I can. I can talk to them and smooth it all over. Chris, you can't just uproot away from me so quickly, there is so much more I need to learn. And fucking tell me how fast is time there already."

"It's okay D, it'll be cool. We aren't leaving tomorrow but we do need to finish the Wrist-Vectortraining." Don did not blink. He was waiting. "Nexus is 4:1 time difference." Don blinked. Conducted math in the air and blinked again.

"Alright. Fine. That's not too bad. Joshua Hills is 3:1 to Earth, and I'll be spending most of my time in and out of here for a few more years. I'll also visit all the time and—"

"No," Chris interjected. "It's 4:1 to Joshua Hills, which makes it 12:1 to Earth," Chris said. Don stared at Chris. Once again, Don did not blink. After an elongated moment, Don slammed both fists into the sink, shaking all the loose dishes and causing the glass to break. He left his fists there and welcomed the pain. He soaked the throbbing pain in and began to breathe deeply. Don raised his hands again ready to slam even harder this time. He swung down but Chris caught both his forearms. Don's momentum was still too fast and although they did make contact with the sink, it was minimal.

"Don, stop! Stop this. It will be okay, I promise."

Don's eyes swelled with tears causing his vision to blur. His eyebrows wanted to curl upwards but Don forced them down to mask his expression. This caused the pool of tears to leak down his face. His nostrils began filling with tear-filled mucus, which was also now dripping from his nose. His skin grew hot and his face blushed red. Chris let go of his forearms and grabbed him by his arms and pulled him in. Chris could feel Don's arms muscles contract with a fit of quivering anger and embraced him even harder.

"Argggh! What the fuck man?" Don asked without really expecting an answer.

"It will be okay I tell ya. I'll just have my future kids make pretend they are us and you'll never know the difference. Honestly, you'll come over, and ill teach my son how to stab you like a pro, and it'll be like old times." Chris held an imaginary blade and began stabbing Don in the ribs.

Don began to flinch away from the fake stabs, and chuckle a little. "That's the stupidest shit I ever heard." Don's voice cracked. His vision was still blurry from the tears but that did not stop him from attempting to stab Chris back. The two gave each other a few more fake stabs before they hugged each other. No pats this time, a full embrace was in order. "You're gonna be an old man soon, Chris."

"I'm going to have a full life. Don't you worry brother. What's that you always say? Our memories will live longer than we do, well it looks like that's definitely the case this time, bud." Chris reached behind him and reveal in his hand a chrome handle with the inscription "RSF" on it. It was immediately apparent to Don that this was his personal Ahir Blade, which is given to a candidate upon completion of their trials, knighting them as an Official Realm Seeker and inducting them into the Realm Seeker Federation, or RSF.

The blade was normally retracted into the crystal handle, which was the same material as the pyramid centered on a Wrist-Vector. The grip was rectangular in nature, with two indentations allocated for the middle and forefinger. The base curved slightly forward, and at the top bolster area, where the blade was retracted in, it emanated a dim blue light. The two finger-wells indentations also served as the blade release switch. While gripping the handle, Chris compressed both finger-wells and the metal blade jolted out with such speed that it produced a recoil sending Chris's hand slightly back. He gave it a slight toss, caught it by the base with his forefinger, and began to balance it. As it teeter-tottered, he extended his arm towards Don and looked him in his eyes. "I want you to have it."

"Absolutely not."

"It's already a decision I have made. It is no use to me now, except to remind me of a part of my life that I am ready to move on from." Chris grabbed the handle again, flicked his wrist and the blade retracted back in. "Just take it before I stab you with it." Chris then gave the air around him a few empty stabs.

"It sounds just like mine."

"Well, there you go, even a better reason to take it."

"Thank you, brother. This means a lot." Don reached out a grabbed the Ahir Blade. He tossed it from hand to hand a few times, creating a smile on both their faces. With a final toss into his right hand, he took it and placed it in the inner side of his right boot. "I love you, old man," Don said and the two laughed.

"I love you, too."

CHAPTER 10

D ayna held Elle's hand as she led her towards the back of the abode. There was a smaller door there, barely visible due to the roots that were surrounding the frame of it. "The boys might be in there for a while. Come hon, I'll do the DNA extract for you. I'm much gentler than Chris anyhow." Elle took a look around the room, which was much larger than anticipated due to the nature of the entrance. The walls were aligned with shelves that contained boxes with odd names labeled on them. She took the time to read some: "Trinskees from Hornell Yards, Buoulbs fallen from the Tree of Yardis, Xe Extract, and Dust of De Ole' Buckchin" were some that stood out. Instead of asking what everything was, she just accepted them for their existence. Opposite to the wall of shelves was a chair that was no different than the ones that were in the living room. Cozy, and appealing in every way, yet still more efficient than comfortable. On the desk next to it was the machinery that was going to be used to extract this DNA of hers. Seemed like a basic blood draw collection point, like the ones used in her hospital. A few more lights and switches than what she was used to, but she was fairly certain she was correct. She began to naturally make her way to it but stopped mid-track once she realized that there was only one chair in the room. "Oh please, here sit." Dayna pointed. "This seat is for you. We actually had no seats here until Don convinced us we needed one. He simply just lugged one here one afternoon, and it has been here ever since."

Elle sat down and placed her arm on the table next to her. "Just blood, is that all you need?" she chuckled.

"Just that and a couple of teeth, my pretty." Immediately they both laughed. "Yes, hon. That is all." Dayna still smiling wrapped a constricting band around Elle's bicep and began to unpackage a sterile needle. She felt for a vein and slide in the needle effortlessly. She grabbed three vials and drew blood until they were all filled. "We only need one vial, but I can't tell you how many times we needed a spare vial after dropping or breaking the first one. We travel to many locations to set up the Wrist-Vector, and the journey isn't always a smooth one."

"I would love to hear about it one day," said Elle. Dayna smiled as she bandaged the arm up. Elle was unaware that the couple had planned on leaving, and Dayna did not have any plans on changing that notion.

"There is something I've been wanting to tell you." Elle did not change her position in the chair, but suddenly she felt like she needed to be sitting down even more. "I know Don has been preparing you to travel through these doors with him, and I'm sure he has been painting quite a lovely picture of unexplored worlds, with much to see amid adventure and exploration. But you need to know that with unknown worlds comes unknown factors, such as inhabitable places that are not meant for every species to be in. Use caution each, and every time you step through the doors." So far everything that Dayna was telling her was making sense. Elle was always cautious, to begin with, she did not plan on changing anything of that just because Don was leading the way.

"I will be," reassured Elle. Dayna did not seem convinced. "I'll be careful, honest." Dayna crouched beside the chair and placed both her hands on the armchair to keep balance.

"It's not just that. You need to be ready to leave him if for some reason there is too much danger that arises. I know it sounds harsh, but you need to prepare for that scenario if it were to become a reality. Everyone who spends some time in Joshua Hills Waypoint realizes this at one point or another. Once someone steps into a realm where it is abhorrently apparent that they do not belong there, the brain conjures infinite hells in the mind, and it could break your sanity." Elle now began to grow uncomfortable. She had just gotten to know Dayna and was unsure if perhaps she was only kidding. Elle switched her weight in the chair but her unease remained. "We all care for Don, and he cares for us, but even he knows that leaving someone behind is a possibility that is not only probable, but likely the longer you spend time here, and it's especially dangerous for Nomads like you."

"Nomad?" asked Elle.

"Outsiders with no proper training. Those don't frequent here much, but there are usually left behind by someone else and are left to fend for themselves. Nomads usually only want to find their way back to their Original Anomaly, but when their hope fades of that dream, they become desperate and violent. They've been known to frequent near the entrances of the worlds they are left behind in, ready to switch places with the first person that walks through."

"Don never told me any of this."

"I'm sure he doesn't want to frighten you, hon. As I do not either. But. Someone has to tell you."

"So. I'm expected to just leave him, or he will leave me in the middle of some dangerous world with no hope to return?"

"Yes," Dayna said coldly. Elle did not expect such a hard affirmation to her question. This made her question everything she knew about this Waypoint, and even about Don himself. Now the questions began flooding in, and she did not know where to find the answers. She no longer knew if she wanted to continue this path. She was confused. She was also coming to the terms that, regardless of her confusion, there was nothing more that she wanted, than to receive her Wrist-Vector and start opening doors. "There's a reason that Realm Seekers usually don't run in teams, and it's because the dangers they face are much more easily dealt with, without the complications of tied emotions." Dayna grabbed Elle's hand. "And you are most certainly an emotional factor in Don's life if I have ever seen one." Elle felt like what she just said was not only a compliment but perhaps even a bit of a threat.

"If certain doors lead to dark or uninhabitable realms, then why doesn't somebody just destroy them?" The moment Elle asked her question, she could feel the word Nomad displayed over her head. She knew there had to be a reason, but still felt that asking such a question was a real Nomad thing to do.

"Excellent idea." Elle was waiting for her to call her a Nomad, but she never did. "The only thing with that is, hon, is that every night while the doors crawl, they heal also. They've been beaten and battered, but as they crawl, any missing pieces regenerate, and any barriers placed on them disintegrate. The only thing that we have seen work is having a Realm Seeker use their Ahir Blade to create the shallowest of nicks on the door. This is the only way we have been able to indicate a survivability status. Usually, right above the handle, there is a checkmark, or an X marked into it, simple as that. Too deep of a marking, however, and the door will heal." Elle looked around at the room as she was attempting to digest this newfound threat.

"Do I talk to Don about this?" Elle asked mainly to herself but was also interested in what Dayna had to say.

"I think you should, but remember this, you can't see what lies behind the doors with your eyes, only with your heart, and if your heart is in peril, so will your body be."

Muffled sounds of laughter and furniture moving around broke the silence between Elle and Dayna. They both naturally looked towards the direction of the sound and while Elle's face was inquisitive, Dayna wore an eased smile. "Alright hon, sounds like our boys are all done fussing around," Dayna said. She then placed the vials of blood into a rotating cylinder and led the way out of the room and back into the main living quarter.

As the two women entered the room Dayna spurt out laughter as she tried to piece what she was witnessing. Chris was jogging around the living room bouncing a huge ball around while Don was making faces in the mirror. "What are you boys doing?" she asked. The two stopped mid-motion, glanced at her, and then with perfect synchronization continued their shenanigans.

"Just celebrating the company while it's still here. Come join the fun, babe" said Chris while waving one hand at Dayna and still bouncing the ball with the other. A warm smile presented on her face as she grabbed Elle's hand and began to skip over to them.

The afternoon came and the outdoors remained peacefully, while the inside of the Abode continued as if it was the only circus in existence. Furniture was shoved to the walls and the moonshine flowed. Games and delicious delights were once again in constant rotation. The four friends had no qualms with the time that day, for it ceased for them entirely; allowing them to take no note of future worries, nor ponder on past insecurities.

CHAPTER 11

The afternoon Sun began its path into the horizon, and the four friends were sitting in the little grass area that patched the front of the Abode. Chris and Dayna were the first to retreat early to start cooking supper. Don and Elle remained sitting a whisper apart and took this time to relax before returning to Earth.

"Don, there's something that has been on my mind and I want to get it off my chest."

"Fine, the answer is yes. I'll show you my rock collection." He rolled his eyes and raised a finger in the air. "But! Only after I shower them, okay?" Don could not resist a smirk that turned into a childish grin.

"For real." Elle's tone of voice immediately changed his grin.

"What is it?"

"Earlier, Dayna called me a Nomad. She said that there were others and that they were dangerous?" Don let out an exasperated groan and threw his body backward to be able to lay on the grass with his arms behind his head. He crossed his feet and stared up into the sky.

"Nomads is the name given to those that are brought here by someone. They have natural talent, much like yourself, to cross realms and interact with Anomaly points, yet they have no formal training. This lack of training often results in their inability to adapt and overcome the various changing environments presented behind these doors. It has been known from a time or two that they get left behind, for the others with actual training to escape and survive."

"Would you leave me?" asked Elle. This was the true question she wanted to ask but was not sure even now if she would receive an honest answer.

"Of course not." Don sat up and look at Elle. "I'm not bringing you into this because you simply can, I'm bringing you into this because I know you can excel and go beyond the simple exploration phase."

"What makes your formal training so important. Not that I am considering it, or that I'm not, but I do want to know more," said Elle

"Well, see. That's it right there. Your desire to know more, learn more and see more. It's all relative to how your mind operates. You have passion for the beyond and we can sense that in you. Realm Seekers have the ability to make rapid connections about the realm they inhabit, and quickly adapt to their conditions to blend in within the population and environment. See, once you step through these doors, or through any other Anomaly, your mind and body not only go through a period of transportation but also cellular reorganization. Your body and mind transform to meet the rules and natural laws of the world you now inhabit. This not only increase your survivability but allows you to see things almost like a local dweller would. This aids in communication and negotiations with the local populace if there is not already some sort of Valerian presence there." Elle turned her body towards his and could sense an increase in her heartbeat. It was evident that Don had a passion for his job, his duty. Seeing him talk like this created an eagerness within herself to stop him mid-sentence and devour him with her lips. On most occasions she would have already pranced on him, however, she wanted to hear what else he had to say.

"So, our cells actually survive these constant realignments?" Elle asked.

"Not only do they survive, but they also thrive on it. The more frequently they undergo this process, the easier it all becomes. The task of adapting only becomes the burden of your mind. and not your physical body. Your mind will naturally resist these changes that are difficult to make sense of. This is the training that many of us undergo and ultimately are tested during the final trials. While Chris and I build your Wrist-Vector, I will also be visiting you, and teaching you techniques to better become more malleable to realm hopping."

"Malleable?" Elle raised her eyebrow. Don responded with his eyebrow raised also, but just a little more exaggerated. Elle slapped his shoulder to cease his mimicry.

"You have already displayed strengths in allowing your mind to adapt to a changing environment while receiving a vast amount of information, which eased your travel here from Earth, but you are capable of much more." Don stood up and offered his hands to her. "Come, let's bid adieu to our friends." Elle reached out a graciously accepted the assistance. She grabbed his right arm and yanked it towards her as she kicked his right foot simultaneously, causing Don to land square on his elbows and let out a yelp, "yeooww."

"That's for earlier." Elle then bent over and slapped his butt as he laid there examining his elbows. Her hand was quick and to the point. To Don, it felt like a bent ruler was just unleashed upon his buttocks. While holding his elbow he rolled onto his side and witnessed him run into the abode.

"Come back! That's not fair." No one heard him as he laid there with his raw elbows, tingling butt, and amused grin. He could hear his friends laugh and then all say their farewells. Dayna stepped out and began to laugh harder.

"If she keeps this up, we might have to trade you for her. She's a keeper for sure," said Dayna. Don stood up as he smiled and chuckled in agreement. After one more round of hugs, Elle joined Don and they made their way back towards the Earth-bound Anomaly Point. Don pointed out that the Sun was nearing the horizon, and the two kicked up their pace. Walking through the hills and fields of doors with Don at her side was much more enjoyable than being on her own, Elle thought. She took this time to soak in the scenery of which she had spent the last two days. Only two days, she thought how surely it must have been longer than just two days. It felt longer than that, it felt like she had always belonged there.

"How much time has passed back on Earth you think?" Elle asked.

"Probably only about an hour. An hour-ish." As the 18 trees that made the Anomaly point began to draw nearer, Don reached out and grabbed her hand.

"I'll see you soon, right?" Elle asked. She rubbed the back of his hand and he drew her closer.

"Soon yes, but only for you. In about two days Earth time. It'll be just around two months for me, but there is a lot to do for me to keep my mission quotas up for Valeria; while also finishing the necessary steps for your Wrist-Vector. I'll send you a message from my TeleQuick and it'll let you know I'm coming in." The two were now standing in the center of the trees as the midpoint of the Sun flashed perfectly onto the Anomaly. Don placed his thumb on her chin and tilted her face sideways. He placed a gentle but purposeful kiss on her cheek. Elle began to feel a vibration from the center of her body. She was unsure if it was from the Anomaly or Don's kiss. Regardless of its origination, she held onto the feeling as long as possible. Soon after, she was gone.

CHAPTER 12

The next couple of Earth weeks followed along swimmingly. Don would visit every two Earth days, and Elle would always be at the Anomaly Point waiting eagerly. She knew that she had only just seen him and that for the Don it has been much longer, but she could clearly feel his longing for her. She felt it in the way he would grab her and pull her in for that first hug. In the way that his hands would grip the nape of her neck as he drew it in towards to kiss her, and she felt it in how he prolonged each kiss with a deep inhale. The weeks went by accordingly, but their relationship grew at the speed of Joshua Hill's time. The training that was being conducted also gained momentum and Don was very much impressed with the amount of knowledge retained, and skills gained each time he visited. They would sit in dark corners and meditate in silence. They would stand at busy train terminals and recite mantras until all other sounds were drowned out. They would fast and drink only water on some visits, while on others they would take several hours eating a small portioned meal to fully experience each flavorful bite with gratefulness. They would sing underwater and hum while running. Each visit brought new teaching or technique. To Elle, she was just hanging out having endless fun with her best friend. To Don, he would let loose and find pure joy in being able to share his world with his best friend.

On his final visit before he disappeared with no communication, Don entered Earth through the AP the most excited Elle has ever seen him. He appeared and hit the ground running towards her. "I got it!" He exclaimed without slowing down his pace. "It's done, we did it!" Don crashed into her body but managed to embrace her and spin her around. He placed his forehead on hers and grabbed her hand. He reached into his pocket and pulled out a Wrist-Vector. It was her, she knew it was her the moment he placed it in her hand. She felt the rush escape her heart and now fill her face. She screamed with joy and he grinned hard. Don slipped it onto her wrist and helped her secure it as they both started to catch their breath. "It's yours," he said. "You're ready." The crystal pyramid glowed and Elle could feel the warmth of it already travel through her veins.

"Thank you, thank you! I can't place this feeling into words. I knew this was the plan but now the day is here and I'm even more excited. Why didn't you tell me it was almost done?" Don just smirked and winked at her. Elle should have known that he always liked to surprise her, and she was sure that he would always find a way to continue to do so.

"Just don't take it off for 24 hours. It needs some time to fully synchronize with you. I'll come back in two days, and this time, be ready to come back with me." Don grabbed her by the chin and kissed her on the cheek like he always did when they departed.

"I will be," she said. "I can't wait."

CHAPTER 13

But wait she did. She waited and waited with no answers, until tonight. Elle returned her mind to the present moment, as she continued driving through the night towards the Anomaly Point. The darkness of the night had begun to lighten a few shades, and she was comforted by knowing that she was on track to arrive at the AP before Sunrise. The phrase "three weeks" kept repeating over and over in her mind. There was something about it that was making her uncomfortable. She already knew that she was upset for his lack of communication, and she already knew that Don should have reached out to her at least a dozen times by now, but those were not the reasons she was currently fixated. She began to consider the fact that perhaps she was worried about him, that maybe something could have happened to his health, after all, it has been a long time since they spoke. Then it clicked. That was it, a long time, it has been three weeks since she had seen him. Three Earth weeks, her mind emphasized. With the time dilation being different in Joshua Hills, she began to calculate how long it had been for Don. She attempted to calculate frivolous equations that she knew held no weight, for she did not fully understand this phenomenon still. It might have been a year or maybe even two, she realized she had no clue.

For the first time since his disappearance, she considered the probability that the feelings that were previously held between them, suspended in their bubble, might no longer exist. This brought a subtle sadness to her, an unease that she had to physically shake off.

She regained her focus and began to scan the Joshua trees once again. Once she came across a familiar group of trees, she slowed the vehicle and began to inspect each tree with more scrutiny. Her attention to detail had been remarkable before, but now she was fighting through numerous emotions all at once. She had to consciously remind herself to stay the course. Once she was convinced that she was in the correct proximity of the AP, she placed her car in park and stepped out. The first few paces towards the 18 group of trees that made the Anomaly Point, were used to shake off the stillness of her legs that remained after driving most of the night. Once her legs regained their standard senses she took off with a sense of purpose. The top curve of the sun peaked over the horizon and everything was suddenly becoming all too real to her. She was going to travel again, going to undergo a journey to this Waypoint that was all too surreal the last time she went, imagine this time. She thought of Chris and his exaggerated robot-bear character. She thought of Dayna, and her loving and supportive ways. She was eager to see her friends again. Then she thought of Don, the man who ignited feelings and passions within her she did not know existed. The man that made her urinate her pants one time from laughing so hard. The man who, grabbed her chin and kissed her cheek every time they separate ways. Don, who care so much for her, and also the man who left her ditched on the side of the planet for an unknown reason.

Elle had made her way to the center of the trees in the Anomaly and sat down on the same tree that she first did with

Don oh so long ago. The crisp air of the morning now filled her lungs as she began to take deep breaths in. The center of the Sun appeared, it aligned with her and a flash of light peered into her soul and she began to travel.

She left Earth.
She arrived at Joshua Hills Waypoint.
This time, the smell of musty wood was the first tangible thing she could place her thoughts on. It was not as potent as her first visit, for which she was grateful. She looked into the sky at it appeared to be high noon. She looked around and everything else seemed to be just as it was before. Two planets, dirt covering most of the ground with a few grassy patches, and of course, the endless fields and hills of protruding doors. One thing was different this time, however. She was wearing her Wrist-Vector. For a moment she felt as if there was a sort of electrical energy being released into her veins from her right wrist where it was worn. This electrical current coursed through her arm and up her shoulder until it washed away right back into the Wrist-Vector. The sensation was neither painful nor pleasant, but rather a numbing and slightly cold wave. Before being mindfully aware of her bearings, she noticed that she had already started walking. She did not give it a second thought, but rather just let her mind remain in the restful state that it was. She knew that she did not know what to expect once she walked into that Abode, and decided that she rather not spend her walk just thinking of endless scenarios. As she made her way through the field and up the same hill she struggled with the first time, her heartbeat began to hasten as well.

Her throat felt a bit lumpy, and her tongue a bit dry,
Her hand slightly clammy, and her pulse a bit high.

She felt the beat of her heart thud once or twice,
Protruding through her skin like a drumming device.
Fear and excitement shared a race for her mind,
Yet nervousness took the crown leaving the others behind.
What was to come next was completely unknown,
All these emotions creating an anxiety cyclone.
She took a deep breath, and then another,
A clearer mind began to uncover.
More and more breaths followed, deeper and longer,
Until there was nothing that she could not conquer.

Elle took the final steps over the hill and felt at ease once she saw the Abode that she once felt very welcomed in. A stillness in her mind was present, and now the only emotion that remained was curiosity. She would have her answers now.

CHAPTER 14

Don saw Elle appear through the Anomaly far, far off into the distance. He could barely make out the figure to be human, yet he was sure that it was her. His shoulder ached and his back stiffened. In the last two years, he has barely made any contact with other life forms, and now he was about to make contact with one of the most important ones. Elle had remained a figure in his mind that was ever-present. Her image and voice would fade over time, but not completely. However, in his dreams, she would appear from time to time in much detail. They would never speak, but they would just embrace each other. He would wake up with her weight being felt on his body until that feeling too would fade away as he continued his day.

As she walked through the fields towards him, he noted his mind racing off numerous times, trying to find the perfect formula to describe the order of events that caused his disappearance. He ultimately decided there would be no best way and would just speak from the heart. Hopefully, that would be good enough. Don paced on the balcony as he sipped his drink. He realized he was pacing too much and walked inside to sit on his bed. He then realized he was too still and needed to move around, so he proceeded to once again pace around. He alternated stillness and pacing frequently until time escaped him, and he heard the front door open.

"I'm upstairs!" he spurted out. He regretted not being downstairs to open the door. The living room was a much more neutral area he thought. Too late, footsteps were heard on the steps and he tried to calculate how rude he was being. He glanced to the balcony and thought perhaps he should just jump off, and make pretend he was not here. That too was rendered silly because all he actually wanted to do was see her again. Besides, where would he go, he thought? Too late for that plan anyhow.

There she was. There she stood.

Still, and elegant, and very much real unlike the dream version of her. She stood there composed, yet he could sense that she was upset. He could also see it in her eyes that she too longed for him the way he longed for her. Don opened his mouth to immediately begin telling her two years with of information, yet all that he was able to manage was a croaked whisper.

"Elle." Don moved to her slowly. He moved each foot slowly from heel to toe. He crept up and he could feel water forming in his eyes that were ready to be released for years now. He has held each one in until now. He had only envisioned Elle, until now. When he was but an arm's length away, he tossed himself towards her and landed on his knees with his arms wrapped around her waist and squeezed. "I've missed you so much," he said with his voice barely audible to her. Elle hunched over to embrace him with both arms. She slowly crouched down and meet his gaze with tears in her eyes as well.

"I've missed you so much," she said as she took her thumb and wiped away the single tear that escaped from

Don's eye. He sighed at hearing her voice, he felt warmth surround him as he dug his head into her shoulder and made his body limp. He was settled in and never had to leave. Never had to let go if he did not want to. His heartbeat at his chest walls and reminded him that he was still alive. Don knew at this moment that he would rip out his heart if she asked for it, for it was already hers.

There, they remained…until time itself lost track of them.

CHAPTER 15

High noon had turned into late afternoon and neither of the two had said another word. They were pleased with each other's company for now, and that was enough. Neither wanted to disrupt the gentle nature of this newly created bubble. They exchanged glances from time to time, but only for seconds at a time. The raw energy between was too intense for any other length of eye contact. Don cooked a light meal as Elle rested by the balcony, staring off into the horizon. They ate in warm silence and even exchanged a smile at one point. With full bellies and rested souls, Elle began.

"Where's Chris and Dayna?" she asked. Since standing at the AP on Earth, this was the first time that she thought of them. Odd, she thought, that she had not encountered them yet. She was sure Dayna would have much to say, especially if it was to poke fun at Don to lighten the moment.

"They left," Don said as he bowed his head down. He was prepared to discuss many things but forgot that this would have to be one of them.

"So soon, so quick, and just like that?"

"It's been two years, Elle."

"Shit, that's right." This hit her hard. Her head now too bowed down. "Dayna mentioned they were moving on, I just didn't think it would be so soon, or rather that I wasn't going to see them again."

"It wasn't supposed to be like this. She wanted to see you numerous times before they had to leave. They both did. She left you a pile of clothes and accessories from her homeworld that she thought you would rather enjoy." Elle looked up and smiled, her friend still touched her heart even though she left. Don looked up and met her gaze, held it for a moment, and shot them back down.

"They stayed longer than they intended to. Chris had to help me fix some things before he left. Eventually, I knew that I couldn't keep them here any longer, so I thanked them and then asked them to leave. I know they are living a happy life now. Much better than being here these days." Elle was unsure of what to make about his comment. "You can stay in their room if you want, I haven't been able to move into it, it makes it all too real. I feel them too much in there. My place is up there by the balcony. Plus, at times makes me feel as if I'll see them again one morning when I walk down." He shook his head. "Stupid. I know, but—"

"No, it's not." Elle reached out and placed her palm on the back of his hand and rubbed it. It was the first time they touched since their hug. Don marveled at how a simple touch of a hand could ease him so. Not just any hand he supposed, her hand. He rotated his palm and grasped her hand. "But Don, I need to know what happened, not to them...to you. Why? What the hell happened?" Elle palmed his cheek and caressed it. "Please, before I stab you in the eye with a fork, what the hell happened?"

Don smiled.

Elle did not.

"The very day I was preparing to bring you back here, we had one of the greatest electrical storms that I have ever witnessed. It knocked out not only this abodes' power and my TeleQuick system but the whole Grid-Iron, which supplies this entire side of Joshua Hills. Chris and I spent weeks searching other Abodes for people to help us make the appropriate repairs, but it seemed like, as usual, everyone had gone elsewhere." Don stood up and walked over to a small desk near the wall that supported only a lamp. He reached into the only drawer there and retrieved a broken Wrist-Vector. He chucked on the table and Elle could see that the crystal had been broken and stained with black streaks. "This is the one I originally had when we first met. It broke the second day of the storm as we were trying to repair the Grid-Iron. The storm hit our area hard, and lightning bolts were making constant contact with the frame of the Grid-Iron. I didn't know my Wrist-Vector was pressed against one of the power converters for too long. It got overcharged, and it burnt to a crisp, along with leaving this scar." He loosened his new device to reveal a healed scar.

"So, you couldn't travel through doors anymore, why didn't you just come to see me on Earth and tell me all that? If everyone else leaves, then why didn't you?" Elle tried to remain firm as she kept looking at his scar. A part of her wished she would have been able to take care of his wound, another part of her could not have cared less.

"We're Realm Seekers, Elle. There's still a lot of what I do that you don't know. We have a duty to our mission, and part of that is to continue mapping the universe and making appropriate contacts. For this to occur I need a Wrist-Vector, which is more than just an aide to travel. It keeps our position known to Valeria, and allows us to call for immediate backup if needed. Building a new one became my new priority that Chris stayed to assist me with. Not only that, we aren't necessarily allowed to leave our assigned post without one. It's for our safety. The only instances Realm Seekers leave their post without one is when they retire, or when they quit. To go off post without one means that there is no backup, and often Realm Seekers are lost in the Universe, never to be found."

"The Don I know doesn't really, do rules, if anything he just makes shit up as he goes. Winging it is your thing. So why go by the book now. What are you not telling me?" Elle's voice was firm, she would not accept his answer. To do so would mean that he could just disappear again at a moment's notice. She was not fond of being abandoned, especially when she had given a large part of her heart already to him.

"It's not that I have to follow all these rules. There's something else, there is something strange about these storms. Not only are they becoming more frequent, but they are also making contact with doors and permanently destroying them. They explode into tiny pieces and never recover. I've never seen a door not be able to heal and repair itself." Don walked up to where she was seating and crotched by her. He placed his hand on her lap and continued. "Elle, most of my peers, my friends that have made their way through this Waypoint have been getting abandoned as these doors were getting shattered. I was tasked with a new mission. Search and Rescue. I've barely been able to recover but only two Seekers in the past two years. Everyone else still hasn't been found or been determined to be dead by now. Deemed K.I.A. It's not safe for us to continue with our plans. I barely know if I'll make it back every time I go through a door, and I simply cannot subject you to that as well."

"Don't you think that's my decision to make dammit!" exclaimed Elle. "You should have asked me to stay here. I could have been with you all this time, helping you! Instead, you just decided to leave me on Earth, wondering what the hell happened to us and our plans?"

"It wasn't safe!" Don immediately was alarmed that he too was now raising his voice. He took a deep breath and placed his other hand on her lap. "You know you're always welcomed in my life, but I'll never ask you to stay and you know that. It's only been a few weeks for you, but for me, it's been years of suffering. Don't you think I would've communicated with you if my TeleQuick wasn't down, or gone to you if my friends weren't all missing and dying? Don't you think I didn't just want to run to you and place my head on your lap until all this hurt disappeared?!" Don dug his head into her hands that were now holding his, and let out a much-needed scream.

The last two years he had never slowed down, never let up from hunting and looking. Compiling lists and leads received from Valeria into routes of searches through the doors. He compressed the last two years into sound waves and yelled continuously into her hands. He let out a yell that came from his core and did not relinquish it until his voice box produced scratching pain. Even then, he continued to scream a soundless scream with his mouth wide open, eyes shut and veins protruding from his neck.

"Don," whispered Elle, who felt his pain escape him as she tried to receive some of the burdens. She grabbed him by the back of his head and lifted it. Don gasped for air after his prolonged scream. Breathing heavy and looking into her eyes, he did indeed feel relief. Elle, without raising her whisper, stated again, "You should have asked me to stay." Without looking away from Don's eyes, Elle reached in and pressed his lips on his. Don tasted her lips and the final wave of tension slide off him. Just a few weeks ago he never thought he would see her again, and then, just a few seconds ago, he thought he could never live without her.

CHAPTER 16

Don and Elle had transitioned from downstairs to upstairs to enjoy the view from his balcony. He spent the next hour talking about some of his last days with Chris and Dayna and Elle enjoyed listening about her friends that she only met once, but once was all she needed for a lifetime of memories. He told her about the excruciatingly long process of building a new Wrist-Vector and about having a team from Valeriahelp him plot courses to search lost Realm Seekers. Elle walked from wall to wall in his room and asked about various artifacts and items that she found to be appealing. He continued delivering different facts and information that all sounded very interesting up until Elle walked over to his TeleQuick system. She tapped around at the different buttons and switches until suddenly she froze still.

"Ummm, Don?" she began her inquiry. "When I texted you from Earth, you responded using this system right," Elle stated. Don paused his speech and nodded. "I thought, you said it was not working." She stated again, with no inflection of it being a question.

"It came online about six weeks ago. I would have contacted you, honestly, but I didn't know what—"

"Six...weeks?" She now asked with genuine

bewilderment. "So, you went about your days knowing...actually knowing that this whatever quick system worked, and didn't once think to reach out to me?" Don stood up to walk over to her. Elle raised her arm with a stiff elbow and palm facing him, signaling him to stop his movement. "Don't". She then was the one to walk towards him. "And if I did not reach out then what? Eight weeks...ten...or would it be months before you would decide to reach out to me?"

Don opened his mouth but was truly unsure of the answer. The fact was that he had begun to not only lose hope in ever seeing her again, but he also began to lose hope in seeing anyone else ever again. Elle drew closer to him and Don took a single step back as he witnessed her anger increase. Elle hit him in the shoulder, but not as playfully as she would usually. "I—I didn't think to—I don't know how to..."

Elle slapped him on his other shoulder.
Don smiled. He felt loved.
Elle did not smile. She punched him in the shoulder.
Don stopped smiling. That one caused a sting.
Elle began to tear. She punched him in the shoulder.
Don smiled again. Elle did not smile.
She raised her arm, and this time was going for his face.

Don caught her wrist and held it suspended in the hair with her fist clenched.

WAAP!

She slapped him harder in the face with her other hand. Another tear fell from her eyes. Don's face began to

77

already redden. He pulled her towards him from her raised hand and wrapped his other arm around her free arm that was next to her waist. She pulled away but Don yanked her back towards him. She punched his lips with her lips, sending his neck back a bit. She twisted free her arm that was being held up and slapped him on the other side of his face. Then, she kissed him again, with force. As she withdrew, her lip was pulled and caught in between his teeth. He would not relinquish her bottom lip until he had both his arms wrapped around her elbows and back. Elle began to squirm and with her lip free she lunged at his neck and bit down. This sent an immediate and intense amount of pain and pleasure simultaneously to his spine. He loosened his grip and she kneed his ribcage causing him to completely let go and take a few paces back.

Don grabbed at his ribs and hunched over, not in pain, but in a preparatory stance. He sprinted four full steps at her and tackled her onto the floor. She instinctively wrapped her legs around him, squeezed his ribcage with her thighs, and locked her ankles together to minimize his movability. As he felt his ribcage tighten, he reached around for her arms and eventually grabbed both of them by the wrist and placed them above her head against the ground.

They had each other physically restricted.

They had each other mentally addicted.

In between the physical push and pull, they locked eyes and could sense one another. Their longing, and their gravitational passion building. He reached down and kiss her neck. She let out a soft sigh as he stretched out her arms even further above her head. Her breast was now compressed by his torso as he continued to kiss her neck. She rotated her neck outward to allow for more surface area to be kissed. With more room to kiss, Don licked her by the hairline and then blew softly on it. The tiny hairs nearby began to raise, and Elle tightened her squeeze on his ribs. While pressing her ankles into his lower back and bending her knees, she drew him even closer to her.

She felt his dick beginning to engorge on her inner thigh. She then felt how moist she was becoming herself. Don brought her arms together and clasped both her hands with his left hand while beginning to slide down her arm with his free hand. He let his fingers glide softly against her skin and then firmly as he reached her shirt. He lifted her shirt and glided his hand up her ribcage. He would then softly let his hand fall back down to her waist while barely touching her skin along the way, and then once again press firmly as he made his way back her ribcage. Elle turned her head to meet his lips and began kissing him with little breaks to gasp for air. While lifting her waist off the ground, she tilted her pelvis towards his now fully erect penis. Elle drew him in even closer and Don inhaled deeply through his nose as he felt her soft mound press against him. The two kissed as their heads swiveled back and forth. Light bites and swirling tongues consumed them as their bodies allowed gravity to assist with their connection on the ground.

Elle ripped away from one of her hands from his grasp and ran it through his hair. Once she reached the back of his head, she gave it a generous tug and his head tilted up. She licked his Adam's apple and then pulled away from her other hand. She grabbed his head with both hands and began to kiss his exposed collarbone. His shirt kept interrupting her kisses, so she eased her thighs off his sides, reached down, and removed it off his body. She took this opportunity as he sat upright, to release more of that physical aggression that remained. She placed both her feet square on his chest and used her strong thighs to not only push him off her but send him stumbling backward.

She jumped onto her feet and began to rush him. He regained his balance just in time to grab her and prevent her from tackling him onto the ground as she surely wanted to repay the favor. They wrestled standing for a moment, until Don squatted down, grabbed both her thighs firmly, lifted her off the ground, and tossed her onto the bed with him falling right on top of her. He landed in between her legs and began to kiss her just as soon as they both landed. He had one hand caressing her face while the other supported his body on the bed. Elle wrapped her arm around his supporting elbow and tugged at it as she took her other arm and pushed against his chest, causing Don to become unbalanced. As his arm flung from under him, Elle thrusted her hip into his and he rolled over onto his back. She rolled with him and was now straddling his waist. A quick smug and proud smile flashed on her face, which was quickly interrupted by Don grabbing her by the shoulders in an attempt to roll her over. They struggled momentarily until Elle placed the full weight of her body center mass on his groin and began rocking her hips back and forth. Don became helpless and lost strength as he melted under her.

He was unable to move as he continued to melt into the bed. He grabbed her by the shoulder and pulled her towards him. He kissed her slowly now and glided his hands up and down her arms which were supporting her on the bed. With her hunched over kissing him and still pressed firmly against him, Don reached inside the armholes of the blouse she was wearing and unclasped her bra. As he brought his hands out of the shirt's armholes, he made sure to bring along the straps of her bra to her shoulders, so they could fall easier. He reached under her blouse, grabbed her by her ribcage, and lifted her until she was sitting upright. He slid his arms upwards and lifted her arms. In one motion, he removed her shirt upwards and while coming down removed her bra. Don sat up and placed his lips on a breast, as he cupped the other with his hand. Her breast felt soft and smooth, with a firmness that could be felt, as well as seen while she moved her body. He could feel her nipple become firm in between his lips, as he squeezed the other with his hand. He encircled one nipple with his tongue as he softly pinched the other between his fingers while simultaneously palming the entirety of it. As he moved his lips from one breast to the other, he left a trail of light kisses along her sternum. He placed a larger portion of her breast in his mouth this time and began to suck on it while tracing the areola of the other nipple. Elle ran a hand up along his spine until she reached his ear and caressed it as she enjoyed the feeling of her nipple being warmed by his mouth.

Elle pressed down on his shoulders and he laid on the bed once again. As she reached down to kiss him, her weight shifted too much and Don could begin to feel himself slide off the edge of the bed a little. He tried to pause her movement and started to say, "Can you move back I think we are going to—"

THUD!

They slid off the bed together.

They landed on the floor together with Don's one hand wrapped firmly across her waist, and the other hovering above her head to protect it from the drawer that was nearby. His upper back and left thigh slammed on the ground, bearing the bulk of the fall. Elle's leg too felt the shock of the impact of falling into the ground, however, at that moment they could not feel any pain. Pure amusement, a hint of nervous shock, and some surprise of not being more injured generated a burst of grand laughter that filled the air around them. They heled each other in the same position as they fell, and after a quick visual scan of each other, they thrust themselves into a more violent barrage of kisses and caresses that was headed straight towards an abyss of bliss.

CHAPTER 17

An Abyss of Bliss

Encapsulated and forgotten is my enamored heart,
Imprisoned frivolously in this emotional case.
Its key unknowingly held by my counterpart,
Only released into the lock by a true embrace.
Before a touch is ever grazed,
The eyes of the souls connect and are set ablaze.
Breath hastens as hands hesitate,
But at that first touch, all worries dissipate.
The notion of time crumbles as walls disintegrate,
And nothing is left but the conjunction of fate.

Kiss by kiss the room swirls into an abyss of bliss

The ridges of our fingertips embark on a journey,
With no mission to end and no sense of hurry.
Caressing each acre of the skin's landscape,
Tracing all crevasses down and up to the nape.
Breathing heavy, and letting passions drape,
Compressed bodies destined to never escape.

83

Kiss by kiss the room deepens into an abyss of bliss

Kiss by Kiss the room becomes an abyss of bliss

Exploring the astronomy of our anatomy,
Suddenly comes the epitome of an epiphany.
Our hands explore with such autonomy,
You are a part of me, even when you're apart from me.

CHAPTER 18

Don laid her back onto the bed and started to kiss her collar bone. He alternated between soft, gently placed kisses, and more purposeful ones as he made his way down the center of her torso. He stuck his tongue out, and continued down a path towards her belly button, leaving a thin trail of moist skin. He then kissed his way towards her right hip and began to bite it gently. She swooned and he bit harder. The space between her lower ribs and her hip was one of her sensitive spots and he ensured to spend some time in her favorite spot. He bit harder under she squirmed away and he continued down. As he passed her lower abdomen, he bit the string that tied her shorts together and pulled them apart. Elle raised her hips and he slowly but surely slipped off her shorts and underwear. The aroma between her thighs was intoxicating to him, he felt her DNA code seep into his nose and was pleased with how it made him feel.

He kissed the inside of one of her knees as he reached down to touch the opposite ankle. He kissed his way up her thigh as he used his hand to lightly trail his fingertips up her other leg. As he centered her core, he pursed his lips and blew soft air over it, and began kissing her other thigh. He did this back and forth a few times until he could smell her aroma even stronger as her mound moistened. With the tip of the tongue as pointed as possible, he licked her up and down along the outside of her labia. Elle would move her pelvis towards his tongue but he made sure not to reach her center yet. He wrapped his arms around her legs and gained better control. He then flattened his tongue as much as possible and pressed firmly on her clitoris and took on a long and firm lick up. He used the tip of his tongue to encircle her clitoris a few times before once again flattening his tongue. This time he pressed firmly against it while pushing and pulling her waist up and down it creating friction that began sending tiny jolts of electricity into Elle's back. Don could now taste her newfound wetness and he drank her in fully. He decided then was the perfect time to taste her completely. He reached around with his hand and placed his thumb on the hood of her clitoris as he entered her with his tongue. As he gently stroked the area with his thumb as he also stroked the inside of her with his tongue. He made sure to taste every wall and every arch of her.

Elle sank into the bed as she tilted and swirled her hips unconsciously. She was forced to bite her lip as she reached down searching for his head. She ran her fingers through his hair and gripped it unknowingly. Don welcomed her touch, and moved his hand from her surface body, to gently sliding a finger inside of her. He could feel the warmth inside of her begin to rise. Now began the power struggle between his finger and his tongue, and Elle gladly welcomed the competition. He alternated between his tongue and finger, while his other hand gripped her waist still. He felt the inside of her while tasting every last drop of her. He reached in and felt the striated fleshy mound that created her G-spot. He applied generous pressure as he encircled the area. Her juices flowed down the side of his face and chin. He became fully erect from the sound of her beginning to purr a low moaning sound.

On the desk beside the bed, was a pair of his favorite drinks. A late afternoon hot tea, and his ice-cold moonshine. With his free hand, he reached over to the glass with ice in it and grabbed one. He plopped a cube in his mouth and let the ice change the temperature of his tongue. Seconds later, he placed his tongue on her navel and proceeded downwards leaving a trail of cold anticipation. He never removed his tongue, and once he reached her opening, he slid his icy tongue in as far as humanly possible. His icy tongue began colliding and merging with her warm core, and it sent a shock of pleasure straight to her heart, leaving frosted goosebumps all along her spine. Don could sense his tongue warming, and retracted it into his mouth to once again swirl the ice cube around. He proceeded to insert and remove his tongue while exploring her insides and constantly reintroducing the cold element. Once the ice cube shrank to half its size, he began a balancing act where he placed the ice cube in between the tip of his tongue and her labia lips. He trotted it up and down until it finally lost balance and slipped to the side of the bed. He took this opportunity to reach over to the nightstand and take a drink from the hot tea. He filled half his mouth with the drink, bearing the heat of it, which he instinctively wanted to spit out. He angled his head upwards, as to not allow the hot liquid to spill out as he opened his mouth and began to lick her now cooled vagina. Once again, the contradicting elements sent an immediate rush to her beating heart. She gripped the sheets beside her and groaned "more" as he continued to experiment with the hot tea, the ice, and his tongue.

Once there was no more ice left, and no more hot tea to drink, Don reintroduced the same forefinger he was using

E.B. WILD

previously. Moments later he slid a second finger in. The change of width and pace his fingers explored her insides, coupled with his flat tongue pressing on her clitoris, sent Elle into a new elevation of sensation. Her eyes were closed but she could see dots appear and disappear. Her mouth was open and could feel the air around her thicken. She had to remind herself to breathe and she constantly held her breath to allow all her sensations to fully infiltrate her body and mind. Her body arched and created distance from his mouth and hands. He pursued. More arching of the body. More pursuit. She swayed her hips and rubbed her tender clit against his stiff tongue. They had crawled halfway up the bed when Don quickened his circulations and insertions of his two fingers, and Elle froze. He could feel her walls stiffen and spasm as only a squeal escaped her mouth. Within her, waves of reformed pleasure built inside her until it was too much to bear. The waves washed over her skin and into her veins, crashing into each other, and continued onto the next set of waves of orgasmic bliss. Don gently leaned over and began to lick her clean as she poured her juices onto the sheets. His attention to her every groan and pelvic tilt began to excite her again as she started to feel a second, smaller orgasm starting to form. Elle mustard what rebellious strength she had and pushed Don away with her knees.

Don was unwillingly removed from the inside of her as she sat up and pushed him down onto his back. Elle grabbed him by the waist and unbuttoned his shorts. His erect penis was painfully pressing against the shorts and began to curve with no room to grow into. Elle slowly unzipped him, releasing the pressed tension of his penis, and removed the rest of his clothes with ease. She gripped his penis and bit her lips. His cock was hard and throbbing like a racehorse's calves at the finish line, except he was just getting started.

She inserted the head of his penis into her mouth and left it there as she swirled her tongue around it so continuously that felt like a hundred times to him. He instantly let out a sharp sigh. She devoured his penis momentarily, completely in her mouth, and sucked firmly as she pulled away. She licked her lips and could feel herself getting wet once again as she looked at Don's face filled with curled eyebrows of pleasure. She continued to stroke him and suck the tip of his head until he was filled with agonizing bliss. He could sense that he was becoming increasingly sensitive to her every movement.

Elle withdrew momentarily from tasting him to catch her breath, Don took this opening to reach down and clasp a hand on her neck and pull her upwards. Being that she was not ready to leave from pleasuring him, she fought back. This tension only created a stronger grip to be formed and ultimately increase Elle's already fast-beating heart. She succumbed to his grip and began crawling her way up to him. Her naked body was dripping over him as she straddled him, and slowly crawled her way up to his laying body. She moved slowly as to not lose her balance, and her neck was stretched out as he kept the tension with his pull. Her head was finally guided to meet his with nothing but an inch apart from each other. Don released her neck and she drew in a long deep breath. As she exhaled, she reached down to grab his penis and guided it inside of her. She drew in another deep breath as it slid perfectly inside of her, opening her up from her core. He resisted the urge to thrust inside of her and slowly allowed her vagina to consume him. She lowered herself steadily like a snake shedding its skin meticulously. The warmth of her insides melted around the girth of his penis and she felt him expand her as she continued to lower herself. Once she reached the base of his penis and her labia rested on his skin, she squeezed her Kegel muscles and gyrated her hips to fully nestle him in. He drew his deepest breath and did not believe he would ever exhale again. His hands slide up her waist and she began to rock back and forth. She rode him wildly and passionately as he explored her breast with his hands. He tried to sit up for a moment to kiss them but was met with a palm to the chest and shoved back down.

Don could feel her weight being shifted to be more supported by the palm on his chest, as she raised her hips and began bouncing her ass on him. The pure ecstasy that was consuming Don was incredible. It caused him to close his eyes and revel at the moment. Being a selfish lover was not a typical trait of his, but to his surprise, it was futile to resist such raw sexual power Elle was exuding. Every time she lowered herself onto him, he let out a forceful breath. Don began to push back and perfectly time his upward thrusts as she came crashing down into him. The noise made by the two bodies crashing and thumping into each other was perfect clapping harmony to their ears. Don placed one hand to where their bodies connected and followed her clitoris with his thumb wherever it went. She began to moan in short intervals as he rubbed her while she continued to bounce on him.

Don could now smell her wonderful scent from where he was laying. It energized him to once again sit up and grab Elle by the waist. She once again attempted to push him onto his back but with a quick twist at the waist, she became unbalanced and fell onto her belly and elbows. Don raised himself to his knees and positioned himself behind her. He placed his hands at her waist and could feel her hipbones protruding out begging to be gripped. He dug his fingers into her waist and pulled her towards him. As his stiff cock gently pressed against her warm mound, he savored the moment by grabbing his dick and encircling her opening with just the tip. Elle tried to press backward to have his shaft enter, but he would not allow it. He was in control of not only her waist but of her sexual pleasure, and he was enjoying it. Don reached around her pelvis with his right hand and began to stimulate her with his two center fingers. Her hips instantly began to gyrate and Don continued to tease her with the head of his penis. Only mere moments passed as this enticing venture took a life of its own, and he thrust fully inside of her in one direct motion. As soon as his pelvis smacked her buttocks, he retreated his inserted member back to only the very tip and thrust once again with all his force. After several powerful strokes, he lifted a leg, bent his knee, and placed his foot on the bed. Without minimizing the strengths of his thrusts, he removed his hand from her center and lifted the other leg. With both feet on the bed, he crouched down and was able to deliver even stronger thrusts while gripping her hips and rocketing them back into him. He fucked her as if he wanted his spine to connect to hers. Her moans turned into tiny screams as he continued to relentlessly penetrate her over and over with no signs of stopping.

Elle stretched her arms forward and lowered her torso until it was flush with the mattress underneath, causing her buttocks to raise. Don looked at her large breast snuggle into the bed and squish into another form. He and watched her ass ripple as he thrust into it. He witnessed her grip the sheets and moan into the corner of the nearest pillow. He was enthralled by the way her body moved and it created his heart to beat and thud against his chest wall, begging to be released. All the blood being pumped inside of him seemed to flow directly to the nerve endings that seemed to engorge the head of his penis even more now. Elle could feel his grip tighten and his breath hasten. His strokes began to slow down but lengthen in stride, and she could feel him gyrate inside of her. His right leg quivered for a moment as he began to moan audibly and call out for her. "Elle..." he uttered out loud, and the sound caused her to squeeze her interior walls and jiggle her buttocks to further entice him. It was the final and ultimate rush that sent him over the edge. He gripped her waist tight, tuning his knuckles white and creating bruises that would not surface until the morning. His left knee buckled as he delivered one final thrust, and released a wave of passion that began at his chest and escaped into her, warmly oozing her insides. His cum pulsed out of him as his cheeks flushed red. He began to feel lightheaded and melted on top of her. She rolled onto her back and took him into her arms while caressing his head that laid on her chest. They both laid there, catching their breaths as the room spun around them.

CHAPTER 19

The afternoon's breeze entered the room slowly, as to not disrupt the stillness that was created within. Two naked bodies laid together with only movements of interlocked fingertips exchanging touches. Neither spoked. Neither needed to speak.

Neither moved, much. Neither needed to move.

The air that filled their lungs seemed to have a different volume quality to it since they could feel each exchange of inhalation and exhalation in detail. Elle closed her eyes and licked her lips frequently, still hearing the sounds of their lovemaking echoed into her head. Don would stretch from time to time, ensuring that his body never left contact with hers. They reveled in the breeze and their empty minds only thought was to simply enjoy hearing each other breath.

They passed a full hour soaked in this glow until a thought entered Elle's mind.

"I want to go through the doors." She spoke this out loud even though it was meant to only be inside her head. She realized that neither had spoken in a while and momentarily regretted the sound of her voice, yet, what she said was something that she felt, and it held true. She repeated herself with confidence this time, "I want to go through the doors."

"You can't be serious, Elle." She was taken back for a

moment since she was not expecting to hear her name said, especially in such a serious tone of voice. She was trying to decipher if he no longer wanted to commit to their previous plans, or if it was truly not safe to go beyond those wooden wonders. "I've spent the past two years fearing each encounter through those doors, and here you lay asking me to go through them?" Don's tone of voice changed from stern to concerned. He stood up, finally breaking contact with her skin, and began to dress.

He was always more about effective casual wear than anything flashy or unnecessary. He preferred shorts and a regular tee shirt. He was constantly on the move and did not want to be restricted by his gear, even less by his clothing. His leather boots had been softened over the years. They fit like gripped gloves for his feet. It was only when he introduced Chris's Ahir Blade into a custom sowed slot in his right boot that he went through a small period of readjustment. He rarely needed it, oftentimes even forgot it was there until he removed the boot. On his gear belt, there usually was no more than a hydration flask, his own Ahir Blade, and some basic survival tools. Some items in that category included: compressed rope, reusable tape, a swallowable lung for breathing underwater, and fire-producing snap paper. He rarely packed more since he knew he had to be back before the doors crawled. Don began to conduct the regular inventory check of his belt and clothes when Elle stood up and walked over to her bag and retrieved her Wrist-Vector.

"I wore this for weeks, waiting for you to return," Elle said as she secured it to her wrist. "Not a single waking hour passed without me thinking of you and this damn adventure of yours." Elle picked up her scattered clothes and started to also dress. "Either you're coming with me, or I'm going alone."

"We aren't going. No more of this, please."

"Like I said, with or without you." Don stared into her eyes, searching for any sign of her bluffing. He was not convinced, yet, he was not dissuaded. He began to pace, not considering going through the doors, but rather how to convince her not to. He began to run different scenarios in his mind when he was interrupted by loud trotting sounds. He turned around bracing himself to see Elle stomping on the ground in frustration, but what he encountered was seeing her run down the stairs with a sense of urgency.

"Impossible," he said out loud. "No way you're actually going to—" He was wasting his time speaking, she was already out of earshot. "Fuck!" He dove into his gear and searched for his items. Luckily, he had his gear belt already set up. He secured his second Ahir Blade, and Wrist-Vectoron, and attempted one last shout. "Don't! Come back," he pleaded.

A waste of time, she was already out the door and speeding into the fields. Don sprinted down the stairs while fumbling to secure his device. He was faster than her, but to his surprise, not by much. Don witnessed her pass several doors, which eased his mind into thinking that perhaps she was truly bluffing.

Of course, she was not. She ran towards a door and gripped its handle. She swung it open jumped in fully committed. He had only hoped she didn't forget to check for an indicating notch on the door. He needed to know if that door was already discovered, but he could not yet see the engraving. His heart raced but it was not due to his dashing through the field, he was worried he would lose her into an unknown realm. He had only gotten her back; he was not ready to lose her again. The door grew closer to him and even though he was squinting his eyes to focus, the speed of his sprint prevented him from seeing any notch. The fear of the unknown began to present itself to him. No notch to see. No notch. His head filled with this thought, which he knew he had to push back. No notch, maybe. Maybe there was a notch.

Steps away and he looked above the handle.

Notch present.

Specifically, a checked notch is present.

The door was cleared previously, and there was no longer any fear remaining. He quickly glanced at the sky to annotate the Sun's positioning,and realized the afternoon was turning into evening. Still hours away from dusk, and even further away from the doors crawling. He scanned the skies for the possibility of a storm and found no evidence of such. No fear remained within him, and he jumped through the door.

CHAPTER 20

Elle jumped through the door and was smacked with thick air, and humidity unlike ever known to her before. Her eyes were blurry from the vibration caused by jumping through the door. She was much more disorientated than her travel through the Anomaly into Joshua Hills Waypoint. Breathe. She did remember to tell herself this. So, breathe she did.

Her vision began to gain minimum clarity and she witnessed a shrubbery of green in front of her. A few more deep breathes and suddenly an expanded spectrum of bright greens to emerald greens filled her peripherals. As her dizziness faded, she peered into a deep and vast jungle with trees that towered over her. She was amazed by what she was seeing. Her lungs expanded to their fullest volume as she took it all in as she inhaled deeply. She could feel her lungs quiver as they morphed into a larger organ, then she felt that same shaking feeling in her extremities. Her hands and feet began to grow in front of her eyes, and she witnessed the skin of her limbs become rougher and thicker. Coarse hair sprouted from her pores. Her shoulders began to broaden, and she could feel the fibers of her muscles begin to rip and grow in size. Her head began to swivel and she witnessed herself morph and change in all areas. She could feel her insides and much as she could feel the wind hitting her exposed skin. Her DNA was altering to adapt to this world and she had never felt this feeling before. It was intoxicating, and she wanted to consume it fully.

She then began to consider the increasing improbabilities of things that could go wrong. She had confidence in herself, but she lacked the training, at least that is what she was told by multiple sources. She began to doubt herself and the morphing of her body began to hurt. The pain was felt across her body and her mind became clouded with more concerns. Her hands shifted back and forth from an ape-like hand to her regular hand. The veins in her neck changed into darker colors as they shriveled and sunk into her neck skin. Hair follicles began to appear and grow sporadically across her body, and then retreat in her skin. Her head began to hurt and pulse with a thick pain that felt like syrup was being poured into her skull. She then felt various groups of muscles being torn apart and then being instantly healed to only become shredded fiber by fiber once again. She let out a yell that turned into a pleading whimper as the pain increased to excruciating levels. She fell to her knees and began to hyperventilate. Grasping at her throat she began to consider that perhaps she was not as ready as she believed she was.

A large shadow appeared from the right side of her depleting vision. She was unsure if it was her brain creating shadowy figures from the lack of oxygen that was overwhelming her, or if she was now in imminent danger for her life. She recalled looking at the notch above the handle before entering and thought it was a checkmark. She could not fully confirm at that moment if she may have been mistaken, and simply rushed in. She panicked more at the prospect that she may not have the ability to defend herself while in that state of vulnerability. The shadow focused more clearly, and she was certain now that it was indeed a creature of that realm. The figure was full of short, light brown fur, that spanned evenly across its body. Its broad shoulders paired with a muscular physique walked on two legs and drew closer. As her vision focused on the figure, she could note that it resembled a cross between a human and gorilla, it also resembled Don, and happened to be wearing similar clothes. His shirt and shorts appeared to hang loosely on him since several rips were surely caused by his transformation. Her breathing began to taper down as she came to the realization that the figure was indeed her dear friend.

Don knelt beside her and placed his heavy hand on her shoulder. "Breathe," Don's voice was deeper but still recognizable, "Breathe deep, Elle." He rubbed her back and it somehow eased the pain. "There is nothing different about this that you haven't done before. Remember, a different realm, same Elle." She closed her eyes and began to repeat this to herself out loud as if it was her personal mantra.

"Different realm. Same Elle."

Deep Breath.
"Different realm. Same Elle."

Deeper Breath.
"Different realm. Same Elle."

Deepest Breath.

A low humming was felt in between her ears and she opened her eyes and saw that her transformation was completed. She stood up and was taller. Still was wearing the clothes she entered with, except there were a few more tears in the seams. The humidity in the air vanished and the air she drew in was rejuvenating. She could feel the strength that laid within her forearms and calves and flexed both muscle groups simultaneously. She looked down and stretched her rugged and callused fingers. She felt inhuman, and she was correct. A different type of strength and power coursed within her. Her DNA had morphed to better facilitate her in this jungle-esque realm. She stood proud and felt home in her new but temporary body. Don stood in front of her amused and delighted to share in her revelry.

"There's nothing like witnessing someone's first DNA morph," Don said. He was proud of her and she could sense that. She looked past him and could see deep into the jungle. Her attention to detail was impressive as she noted all the moving creatures and subtleties of her new environment. She wondered if she always had a vision this impeccable, and quickly realized she had not. Whatever creature she had adapted into was superior to humans in numerous ways. She took a few paces forward and felt the earth underneath her cushion her naked gorilla feet. She dug her toes into the soil as if she was on the beach. She curled her long toes and gripped the now compacted ground as she prepared to take her new legs for a jog. She pushed off the ground and was propelled forward with a force that surprised her. Instinctively her other foot landed on the ground in front of her and propelled her even further. She quickly advanced her trot into a full-on bi-pedaled sprint. Not only was her vision able to scan her surroundings with expeditated accuracy, but her senses were also heightened. She could smell the location of fruits around her, taste the scent of the freshly moved ground below her feet, and feel the wind swerve between each strand of hair.

As she sprinted through the jungle, she was focused

on the path that not only laid in front of her but much beyond in front of her. She began to focus on the path further out and a new, more animalistic urge arose. She wanted to just jump into it, and lunge at the path ahead of her, and so she did. She leaped into the air and dove forward. She landed on the knuckles of her hands and they dug into the ground as her thighs touched her chest to prepare for the next full leap forward. Her legs ejected her into the air once again, but this time she landed more horizontally. With her torso tilted to one side, and dominant shoulder forward, she had now gained even more speed than when just using her lower limbs. A rhythmic pattern of trots and stomps marched through the endless forest. Elle laughed at the amount of pure joy that overcame her, and a tear fell from her eye.

She continued to rummage through the jungle, creating new paths on a whim as she spontaneously willed it. Leaves began to fall ahead of her and the sound of rustling branches grew. She scanned ahead but it wasn't until she looked up that she noticed what was the cause of all this. Don was swinging from the branches and jumping off the sides of trees, chasing her around as she explored her new abilities. She hadn't even thought about him as she sprinted off, but she was sure glad that he knew better, and was not too far behind. Having him there provided a sense of comfort that she needed to fully let go. She felt safer with him nearby. She always had.

Her instincts once again took command as she leaped upward a few feet onto the side of a tree. She cushioned her high-speed impact by bending her knees and almost immediately springing them up and launching herself to a new height. She continued to propel herself upward until she was able to reach the branches near where he was swinging. She reached out and gripped the branch with a single hand. Only for a brief moment was she worried that she would slip and fall the dozens of feet below her. Once she felt how natural and powerful her grip was upon that branch, the only thought that remained was to catch up to Don. She swung from branch to branch, half focused on Don's trajectory, half still bewildered. Perhaps if she was fully focused, she would have noticed that he had slowed his pace and was intentionally letting her catch up to him. Don kept his eye on her, and when she attempted a large jump for a branch right below him, he ceased swinging and fell on top of her. He gripped her forearms with his feet and caught onto the branch she was originally aiming for with both hands. She remained suspended in the air, held only by his feet.

"I could let go, and you could fall who knows how far. Keep present and focus on your immediate surroundings. That is how you will continue to survive." Don smiled at her but was also stern with his voice.

"Seriously? Is this the best time for—" Elle realized that this was the first time she spoke since crossing the door. Her voice sounded different. Sounded deeper and it amused her. She chuckled at this and he misinterpreted this as a lack of concern for what he was trying to teach her.

"Very well then," he said and let go of one arm. Elle gasped and began to swing wildly for anything to grab onto. There was nothing nearby. She did not panic as her eyes scanned the area eagerly. She kept looking until her eyes finally found a tactical advantage.

"You. Pick me up!" Elle said. Don laughed, and it was clear that he felt in charge.

"You're going to regret that laugh if you don't pick me up this instant." Elle's voice was lower and even gnarled as she spoke this time. Don didn't budge. Before he had a chance to consider any other options, she reached up his shorts and grabbed his exposed testicles. Don tensed and almost dropped her out of sheer shock. This shock turned rapidly into fear. Fear that she would plummet down, testicles attached to her grip.

"Whoa, whoa...easy. Easy" He whispered and spoke much softer now. He moved even slower with his other leg and clasped his toes around her wrist. He pulled her up so she could now also grab the same branch. They remained hanging there, face to face, Elle still cradling his balls. Don started to become aroused but still refused to move. Elle was in full control now. She loosened her grip and undid the belt and button to his ripped shorts. It fell to the branch below, along with his gear belt. She slid her hand up the shaft of his different, but familiar penis. She stroked him slowly and smoothly for she was unsure of her newfound grip strength. Don, now fully erect and yearning for her to be closer, let go of the branch with one hand and gripped her by her butt. He squeezed it firmly, and she lifted both legs towards him. She wrapped them around his waist and pulled him easily towards her as they remain suspended in the air. Her grip strength was still fully intact on the branch above. She continued to stroke him and his respiratory rate increased. She wanted to see how fast she could get him to breathe, which was indirectly also turning her on. She wanted his throbbing cock inside of her and she wanted it at that very moment, not caring that they were both only holding on to the branch with only one hand each. She tilted her pelvis up and bent her knees to draw him inside of her. As his penis approached her, he could already feel the heat radiating from it. He entered her directly, and with purpose. She dug her heels into the small of his back and pushed him further inside of her.

As instinctively as running through the jungle on all

fours, she bent her knees more, placed both her heels on his buttocks, and grip them tightly with her finger-like toes. She reached up and grabbed the branch with both hands for more control and began to push him out, and then completely back inside of her. Don caressed her muscular ape butt and assisted with the thrusting motion as he felt her insatiable grip continue to have most of the control. Their bodies began to sway as one while hanging from the treetop, as the unmistakably clapping sound of hard lovemaking shook the leaves around them. What started as slow intentional thrusts, escalated to impossible fast ape-like penetrations that vibrated both of their vertebrae. Elle tilted her head backward, reveled in the ecstasy, and began banging on his chest with her first. She grunted deep animalistic groans as he thrust into her and she pounded on his chest a few more times before almost losing her grip and returning that hand to the branch. This intense passion resulted in the overall grip strength of the two lovers declining. Palms were no longer in contact with the branch, only their fingers remained to cling on, and were the only things separating them from life and death.

They were on their last moments before falling to the jungle floor, but they continued to thrust with no remorse or concern. Don began to sense the engorgement of the head of his penis and the familiar increased sensitivity of it.

He was moments away from death. He was moments away from cumming.

With only one hand on the branch, and the other still gripping her ass, Don had no choice but to continue to be consumed by her, and to continue until completion. The grip of the very tip of his fingers began to leave, and the very tip of his penis began to cum. He held his breath and with his final breath, released a grunt of eternal ecstasy. He slipped from the branch and fell backward into the air below him. He threw his hands back and closed his eyes and accepted his new fate. Don stopped falling and remained secured wrapped in Elle's legs. She never let go of him as he remained inside of her, still ejaculating. Elle had both hands still on the branch above, but they were beginning to lose strength quickly, now that Don laid swinging in the air below her. With his arms and legs extended, her pussy and legs were literally the only things saving his life.

Don began to regain his headspace and was no longer so lightheaded. "Swing me over, babe," he said as he pointed to the nearest thick branch just to the left of her. She started with a few preparatory swings until finally having enough momentum to release him and watch him land. Elle pulled herself up and laid on the branch, catching her breath and basking in the knowledge that Don was ready to choose death over her sexual prowess. She giggled at this thought, and from below Don shouted "I can hear you giggling up there, you know," and commenced to chuckle himself, for he knew what she was thinking.

Elle caught her breath as he began the search for his fallen shorts and a gear belt. She saw that he was busy with his task at hand but patiently waited for the talk she knew he wanted to have with her. She knew that he would have had some stern words about responsibility and being careful. Words about not going through the doors and blah, blah, blah. She knew it was because he cared and was worried, and she had already played out the entire conversation in her head. She was not against having this conversation, but what she was against, was having this conversation at that time.

She decided she would keep this party rolling.

A sudden rush of excitement caused her skull to tingle. She glanced at Don and saw that he had found his shorts. She knew that she had to act fast if she was going to gain a lead ahead of him, and reach the next door. She gripped her feet securely into the branch below and squatted down, preparing to leap. She resonated with the fact that she had so quickly felt at home in this morphed body. She thought back to all the training she had conducted with him and started to believe that perhaps, she was a natural at this. That perhaps, she was built for this.

"Elle?" Don asked.

"Oh, Shit." she thought.

"Come meet me on the ground," he said. Elle reoriented her focus to the path ahead of her and leaped forward with great ease and strength. She laughed as she imagined how in awe his face would be as she so blatantly disregarded his words and sprinted away. A few trees-hops away and she began to swing freely from branch to branch, just like she would monkey bars in the playground as a child.

Don witnessed her leap away and was in so much disbelief, that he was confused on why she would be taking such a long route to get to him. Perhaps she had not fully gained comfortability in her new form and was taking a longer, safer route. Then he thought about the performance she had just executed and knew she had fully mastered her change-over. Then, the lightbulb clicked. "Are, you, fuc-king-kidding-me!"

He squatted down and felt his ape-quadriceps contract into solid stone before he leaped forward. He jumped further than he ever had in this form, yet nowhere near where he wanted, or needed to catch up to her. He opened his mouth to tell her to come back, to explain to her how serious of a mistake she was making, yet all that came out was a roar that bellowed from deep within him. The sound echoed to reach Elle's ears and she became slightly unsettled, but was committed to her actions and kept going. She reached the door and leaped back into Joshua Hills Waypoint.

CHAPTER 21

Furious and angered, Don's neck veins seared and pulsed with fire. Worried and concerned, his eyes glazed over. He began to envision Elle at the Waypoint, already making her way into another doorway and leaving no trace of her path resulting in him losing her forever. His mind distracted him and kept producing unpleasant imageries of her being lost and endangered. He quickly recognized he was becoming overwhelmed and started drawing in deep breaths. The clouding images began to dissipate the closer he gained to the door. As he reached the door, he remembered that he had believed in her since the moment they met. There were numerous reasons he felt gravitated to her, and he tried to find resolve in this. He wanted to believe that she was on the other side waiting for him.

He opened the door and returned to the Waypoint.

She was not there.

She was not waiting for him.

His eyes violently scanned the immediate area. His scan yielded no results. He had no sense of obvious direction, or sound thought towards which direction she may have gone.

"Don't worry, babe!" Elle said from an unknown distance. Don aligned his vision to where the sound was reverberating from and once again did not see her. "This door got a checked notch!" Elle was half into another doorway and waving to him. She was barely visible once Don located the appropriate door to focus on.

"Just wait a minu—" She walked through and shut the door behind her. Don stomped on the ground with his right foot as he regressed into the basic emotion of stubborn frustration. At least she checked for the notch he thought, as he made his way to it. Pacing towards the door, he began formulating a plan in which he would find her, grab her, and if need be, drag her back to his abode. This would be the end of her rebellious adventure and the start of her being safe. Or so he hoped.

He grabbed the doorknob, verified the checked notch, and swung it open. The familiar vibrating hum filled his mind and body as he stepped through. Fractal patterns emerged and disappeared. Don had traveled through anomalies for years and it felt like blinking to him now. A long, strange blink, but nonetheless, a process he was comfortable with. As talented as Elle was, he was sure she was still working through the mental blocks and kinks that came along with this form of travel. This was his advantage to gain distance on her, just like he had in the Jungle when he found her struggling mid-morph.

The first thing in this previously visited realm that he noticed was the smell of salt. This led him to quickly deduce the different possible worlds he could have traveled to. He could not recall a realm where he could not manage well, and also smelled like salt. So, his mind eased, his eyes gained focus, and revealed he was underwater. Underwater was not the right term however he thought, since the entire realm was that of water. There was no above water to be in, just water to exist in.

Before looking at his morphed body, he stretched

E.B. WILD

hard and deep with both mind and body. This technique was one he learned in the academy and was deemed as one of the best techniques to fully conform to his new morphed anatomy. This was a standard operating procedure for Realm Seekers, and it always proved to be of great use. As he stretched, he took in a deep breath and immediately noticed that the oxygen exchange was not occurring through his mouth, but rather gills that were in his neck. He reached up and began to refamiliarize himself with the pair of breathing slits located on each side. The larger breath he drew in, the larger the gaps in his neck opened. He also made a note that his hands and feet were interconnected and webbed. His skin was a combination of regular human texture, but with a hardened, shiny scaled feature to them. His thighs still had a notable separation to them but were joined from the knees to ankles, by means of skin and scales being fused together. They tapered off with transparent fins that extended sideways past his heels. He was very flexible and comfortable in his morphed sea-body and wondered if Elle had been as well. His clothes seemly disappeared from him, but his gear belt remained secured around his waist.

Don swerved his body, flexed his finned feet, and began swimming the waters in search of her. He no longer noted the smell of salt or fish in general. His nostrils and gills were much more attuned to the different species of mammals and coral life that now surrounded him. To him, it felt as if he had a Rubik's cube of olfaction abilities. Being able to differentiate between what could possibly be food, and what could potentially be the looming danger of a larger prey was a huge asset, yet he was unsure if it was too much for Elle. This type of sensory overload could often be a distraction to new travelers, preventing them to decipher and sort out the different priorities of the information being received. He

110

REALMS OF LUST AND LOVE

swam with a sense of urgency and was sure to engage all his muscles. He did not smell any blood, nor did he note any signs of disrupted coral life around him.

Just as soon as he felt that no progress was being made in his search, he became stuck and was unable to swim any further. His arms were free, but his feet were bounded somehow. He curled his body to look behind him and saw that his feet had a roped tied around them. At the other end of the rope, was Elle, pulling tight and laughing hard. Her gills were expanding and contracting so much that Don could see the blue vessels inside of them from where he was. Before he could make much sense of when and how she had bested him, Elle had already tied the rope to a large sea boulder. He swam towards her to stop her from pulling tight on the knot she created, but it was too late. She had secured the knot and already swam away by the time he reached the boulder. He floated there, suspended in the water with astonishment. All along he had been worried about her being overwhelmed and distracted by her senses when it was Don who was consumed by his. He was used to being mostly alone for the past half-decade that he was living in Joshua Hill Waypoint. He was able to always focus profoundly during his explorations, but now his attention had narrowed in on another and protecting her so much that he lost focus on protecting himself. A lesson learned, and taught by a Nomad no less, he thought.

"Your face is priceless. Priceless!" Elle curled her feminine and shiny sea-body and continue to hurl in laugher. "I didn't think that was going to really work." Don swam short distances back and forth. Even when there was no ground to walk on, he managed to pace while he centered his thoughts.

"So, what is your plan here, Elle?" He squared his shoulders so that he was facing her straight on.

"None, there is no plan." Elle stayed at a safe distance from him, knowing that he always had a trick or two up his sleeves. She was on high alert to not be lured in. Don swam forward until the rope was fully extended and there was no slack left. "I know you're upset that I just ran off, but I won't release you until you promise that you're no longer mad." Elle's face shimmered with sorrow. Her new skin reflected emotions by emanating different levels of light from in-between her scales. Instead of blushing, her face grew dimmer, and a pulse of light reflected from her chest. Don was certain that she was unaware of this feature and therefore was less apt to conceal her emotions and her inner light. Don was a bit surprised to learn that she simply wanted him to forgive her for her recklessness and just move on. Typically, his scaly skin would reflect his angered surprise with a vibrant light near his arms, indicating that his fight or flight response system was geared towards a fight. Yet, he remained calm, and no light protruded his skin.

"You think it's that simple?" Don swam forward in a sprint, being instantly tugged back. He had forgotten his bind. Or rather, he wanted to make it appear so. As he was yanked backward, he left some slack in the rope, enough that Elle did not notice. "You placed yourself in danger by just going through the damn doors, to begin with, and then you gave no thought to whether it was safe. What if the door gets disintegrated while we are still here?"

"There was no storm."

"What about the status of the door?"

"There was a checked notch, indicating a safe and habitable status."

"And you have no regards to when the doors will crawl."

"No need, I turned on the return sequence indicator

on my Wrist-Vector."

Don was upset. He was frustrated because she had indeed been prepared, and he was too worried about her safety to realize this. Still, many more risky scenarios could perpetuate danger. It was safer for them to return. "Fine, it does seem that you have thought out some things, but not all things. We should return. Come release me and we can be on our way."

Elle swam closer to him, relying only on her hips to swirl her body as she swam. "But I want to stay." She lowered her head slightly and realigned her eyes towards him. She tried to seductively gain his approval. It was working. Her big eyes were even larger in her mermaid-esque form, and he had a weakness for them. His eyes met hers and he was captivated. His inner glow began deep between the scales of his skin, and Elle, for the first time noticed this light. She was also captivated. She was drawn in by it and steadily began to drift closer to him. He had allowed himself to feel enamored in hopes of this very occurrence. As she drifted towards her, he inched his right hand from his side, up and behind his waist. He was careful to make his movement unknown to her, but she was memorized by the light and wouldn't have noticed a lion with wings swim by. He ran his hand along his gear belt until he found his blade and gripped it. He placed his two foremost fingers on the indentations and waited. He waited for her to get close enough.

She drew slowly, but eventually came in so close, that even in the water he could smell her breath. This signaled him that her distance was optimal. He compressed the blade and out extended the blade in its typical compartmentalized order. The impermeable metal clicked out with force all the way out until the final click was heard. He swung the blade downward while simultaneously reaching forward to grip her right wrist, with his left hand. He cut the rope binding his feet and swung her around, never losing contact with her wrist. His left forearm laid across her chest and he pulled her in tight as he raised the blade to her neck. "I rather think it's time we return," Don said and pressed the edge of the blade on her neck so she could feel the steel.

"And I, rather think it time we stay and play. We only just got here." Elle pressed forward with her neck, creating the blade to now press firmly against her skin and causing an indent. "I'm not going anywhere, and you know that." She took her free hand and reached behind him and began to caress his hamstring muscle. Don shivered off pending goosebumps and attempted to regain his resolve.

"It's safer to return, and if I have to tie you up and drag you out, I will." He raised his blade welding elbow and pressed more tightly across her chest. She gave out a gasp as her lungs were forcefully compressed. Elle seemed to know that he would not draw blood. So, she did. She lifted her neck and slid it across the blade. She winced as a paper-thin red line emerged on her neck. Her blood trickled out of her neck and the surrounding water carried the droplets away. Don instantly retracted the blade back into the grip and holstered it into his gear belt. Across his entire body, his inner light drew grim and dark. For a moment he thought that he had done that to her, that he drew blood. He released his grip on her and she turned around to face him. She raised her hand to his cheek and gently palmed it." Then do it." she said. He didn't move, and he did not know what to expect next. She had just surprised him with her recent display of obvious resentment in returning the Waypoint. She was clearly willing to bleed in order to continue exploring.

She turned back around and began to swirl her butt on his groin. She grinded on him and pressed into him firmly. He became distracted once again, and this time not by choice. He could feel his inner light grow warmly within him, and it began to shine through as his erection grew. He was turned on by how she had turned the tables and seem to somehow be in control. He had to regain it somehow. He didn't need to think very long for she had said it herself. "Then do it." he heard her voice in his head repeatedly. He took the cut rope and slid it across her waist. She never stopped grinding on him, and once she felt his erection press onto her, she only gained momentum. He tied a single knot across her back and left it snug. He quickly created a two-handed handcuff knot and slipped both her hands through them. These, he pulled tighter than just snug. As he synched the rope, he placed his palm square in between her shoulder blades and pushed forward while yanking back on the rope. She was bent forward, and light emanating from between her thighs. They were already naked but as they become both more and more aroused, the scales around their groins began to move apart. Out from under them, their sexual organs were fully exposed with a pulsating light emerging around them.

Elle's tied arms were raised above her back and she was fully bent over. He removed his hand from her back, placed it on her hip, and began to pull her by the rope. His penis glided smoothly into her. Regardless of the surrounding water, he could feel how wet she had become. While maintaining a constant pull on both her waist and the rope, he used the momentum of his floating body to thrust into her relentlessly. She began to immediately moan from combined feelings of pain and pleasure. The rope yanking at her wrists, and her shoulder muscles being pulled backward generated a slight pain response that heightened her senses. The constant thrusting inside of her allowed those heightened senses to be filled with pleasure until they overflowed into the space around them. Don's body was unrestricted by the normal gravity he was used to, and he used this to his advantage. He swerved his entire torso to generate momentum into his back and hips, which he then centered all that power into pleasuring her. As he would thrust into her, he could see the light from himself being transferred to her and ripple from their connected bodies, up her back, and along her spine. These waves of light glowed a particular strength, for they were filled with passion and ecstasy.

Don reached around from her waist and placed his center two fingers on her clit. He pressed and rubbed her, he pulled and entered her, he swirled his fingers and swerved his body. His stiff cock propelled by his strong thighs pumped into her slick pussy with no signs of stopping. The light being generated between them began to grow stronger and changed into more of a charged glow as both of their sexual organs increased in their sensitivity. He had to grab the rope with both hands, and he began to feel the eruption build within him. Elle tilted her head back and open her mouth as if to scream it nothing came out. Don could feel the tightening of her pussy as he witnessed the light from her core begin to pour out of all corners. Usually only one of them came first, while the other devoted themselves to the other's pleasure, but due to their inner lights glowing and moving through their bodies, they were able to synch into each other.

Their lights merged to the point where their origination was indistinguishable from one another. An explosion of light illuminated the region blinding them both, as they simultaneously began to orgasm. Their light cascaded upon all surrounding features, and it extended deep into the ocean planet. Don continued to thrust as he came, while her body trembled and shuddered. His continuation extended her orgasm until they we both fully immersed in the blissful orb of light they created. They couldn't see or feel each other as the pinnacle of their joint orgasm was assimilated by the orb. They remained conscious enough to only feel the presence of one another but not much more.

As the orb shrank, only the sound of slow and deep breathing was heard. Their light gradually dimmed, the water around them settled, and they were both holding onto each other, laying on the seabed. They faced each other while their eyes remained closed. Don caressed her face and traced all her features with his fingertips. Elle held onto his shoulders while rubbing her thumb on its top curve. Don was conflicted and unsure on how to proceed. It was unsettling to him, the amount of unknown harm that could potential occur to her as they ventured through these realms. She was a loose cannon at times, but steadfast and calculated also. Nothing about the way she had been conducting herself would indicate that she could not handle herself. She may have struggled with her first morph, yet the overall execution of her second one seemed to be flawless. She had gained her bearings and adapted to her environment in an expeditated fashion. So much so, that she was able to gain an advantage over him. He wanted to keep her safe, but he also wanted to please her. It seemed as of late, pleasing her was all that he was concerned with.

"Fine," he said. "One more." He placed his webbed hand on her face, and she opened her eyes. "One more door and then we—" Elle lunged forward and kiss him hard.

"Yes! Thank you, thank you. Let's go right now." Elle's face literally lit up with her inner light as she was surprised to hear him speak those words. "Before you change your mind." She twisted her body and sped towards the door, with Don following close, right by her tail.

Off in the distance, protruding from the seabed was the door leading back to Joshua Hills Waypoint. At the base of the door was the same dusty gravel and earth that was found at the Waypoint. Its chemical makeup was unaltered by the water. These doors seemed to exist independently from whatever source was around them. The closer they got, the louder the door vibrated in their ears. They passed through and were once again walking with their own set of legs on the ground.

CHAPTER 22

To Elle, it was eerie how quickly she returned to her original body, both physically and mentally. It seemed that the form she was recently in, not a mere 5 minutes ago, was a distant memory. She could only recall swimming with her fins as if she had dreamt it all, she was now staring at her hands, searching for the webbing that once existed. She reached up to her neck to feel around for any gills, she was not expecting to find any, but she wanted to recall their placement and perhaps remember a little better what it was like to breathe freely underwater. She looked over to Don and shrugged. "Where to?"

"This way, babe. Follow me," he said. Elle smiled and happily followed him. Her hand still assessing her neck region, and her mind centered on that singular word. "Babe." He had called her babe before, but as of late, the word had resonated in her mind with a lingering persistence. She liked the way it sounded, she preferred it even at times. This entire experience had changed her perspective on a lot of things, but mostly her relationship with Don. She often caught herself thinking of him and imagined different conversations that they would have. She was growing fonder of him and his world. She started feeling that she belonged not only near him but near his line of work. There were numerous things she wanted to discuss with him, different emotions and ideas that were floating around in her head since arriving back at the Waypoint. This all would take some time to sort out, so instead, she focused on the next door.

"There is one realm I think you would enjoy very much. I was going to wait until our third or fourth trip, but...as surprised as I am to say this, I think you are ready for it." Don said and pointed off into the distance a mere 200 yards away.

"What type of realm is it?"

"C'mon, babe..."

"Okaaaaay. It was worth a try." Elle knew that anytime he had planned something, which was most of the time, he would rather keep it a secret as long as possible. He would tell her how not knowing only made it better. And he was right. Always right. The suspense leading up to his plans would excite her. Then, more importantly, not knowing what to expect or what was next allowed her to be very present in the moment. Allowed her to soak in all of her immediate surroundings and emotions. This, of course, was the purpose of all that, which he later revealed in one of her later lessons. Being submerged in the present was something she often lost track of by worrying too much about the future, or dwelling on some past event that had nothing to do with her current life. Still, old habits die hard and there was something safe about knowing what the future had in store, but being safe was no way to live.

As they walked towards the intended door, the Sun began to dive into the horizon and the night sky began its journey into the sky. Some of the stronger and brighter stars began to appear and Don explained how most of those were planets. She gazed upon the sky with splendor and momentarily forgot where she was. She felt her feet walking the path, yet, it also felt as if she was floating and being drawn towards them. She felt peace, inner peace, and calmness. She felt the air travel from in front of her and slide into her lungs, causing her chest to expand. She was about to suggest that they wrap the night up and just lay there until the doors began to crawl, but he announced their arrival to the next door.

"Before we enter, I want you to remember to have no fear. Instead of being afraid of anything that unexpectedly occurs, or seems too weird and becomes uncomfortable, I want you to focus on it. Any scary thought of sight you may behold. Focus hard on it, investigate it, break it apart and study it fully. Hone into every minuscule detail, and then little by little start taking control of it, and warp it into something, anything else. Once you observe the feeling for what it is, as just another temporary and interesting feeling, you need to move on and be in charge of your next emotion. Do this, and you will morph rapidly and accurately."

"Well, thanks for the pink-elephant thought, but yes, I will try my best." She turned and faced the door head-on. She was ready to take that first step when Don grabbed her by the chin with his thumb and gave her a firm but soft kiss on the cheek. She looked at him and felt warmth encourage her heart. Every time he looked at her like that, with proud love and a deep understanding of her soul, she felt invincible. She closed her eyes and soaked in his vision. Never would she have imagined that she could feel light-headed, and light-hearted simply from a glance. Yet, here she was about to enter an entirely unknown realm and was holding back her steps to linger a bit longer in this moment. A blissful smile lifted her face and eyes, she took a deep breath and opened the door.

Not half a second later, she was in the air, thousands of feet from the ground, whirling around and plummeting straight down.

Her vision was blurry and could not determine in what direction she was heading, nor where she was. Since her eyes were of no assistance, she decided to shut them. She used her remaining senses to try and sort out any information she could gather. She could not hear anything except for a persistent earthquake that rumbled with great force in her eardrum. The constant reverberating in her eardrum would disrupt any thought patterns that were trying to emerge. She was falling, she knew that, but not much more. One of her priorities now, revolved around overcoming the sound of wind in her ear. She regressed to what she was taught, and to what worked for her most of the time. She took a deep breath in.

Did not work.

She opened her mouth to draw a breath but was met with an unstoppable fist of air that never retreated. She began to gasp and flail her arms around, attempting to grasp for anything that could slow her down, or help in any type of way. Aid was not found, instead, she was met with the inability to control the movement of her arms. With no control and no sense of an improving situation, she was getting frustrated with looking like a fish out of the water, just flopping around. At least that fish would have its eyesight she thought. She curled into the fetal position to at least stop her limbs from flapping around.

With her knees pulled into her chest, she wrapped her arms around them blocking most of the wind, and with her head tucked in, she was finally able to get a controlled breath. A few controlled breaths turned into a deep one, which turned into several deep breaths. Her breathwork turned into a purposeful and rhythmic pattern, and even lessen the harsh sounds of the pounding wind. She was falling faster than before due to her posture, but she felt more of control of her body at least. She opened her eyes cautiously, to analyze if there had been any changes since her last attempt to see. Although there was still a lot of wind irritating her eyes and causing them to water, she was able to see the blurry ground underneath her, through her knees. She managed to decipher that the ground below was mostly green vegetation, and still a great distance away.

She could feel her mind getting cluttered and distracted again by this newfound information. She knew she had to sort out these changes to complete whatever morph was necessary to survive, so she closed her eyes and focused on her breathwork. She curled further into a ball and started to feel her back muscles stretch. Except for the stretch never ceased, and the initial tensions released by the stretch were now turning into a painful pull. She attempted to loosen her back and return to a more upright position, but her body became tense, locked, and unmovable. She began to feel as if the back of her ribcage was growing and pushing through the muscle fibers of her back. This was not a metaphor, for it was truly happening to her, and once she realized this, she began expressing her pain through a low humming grunt. Her skin began to tear apart as her ribcage expanded through the surface. Her ribcage was not only growing visibly outside her body, but it was also creating new branches of bone that expanded horizontally.

The protruding branches of bone began to expand on both sides as her back continued to rip apart creating agonizing pain. She had forgotten that she was still plummeting down towards the ground, and only the pain tearing her back apart remained. She focused on the pain and honed in on where the pain was the strongest. The pain began to infuriate her, it overwhelmed her senses. She began to feel nauseous with rage, her muscles tightened, tears began to fill her shut eyelids, her arms tucked into her chest with her fists balled, and her biceps quivered as she shook with unequivocal wrath. Her entire body started to become numb, but her hamstrings and calves cramped as she deepened her fetal position.

Her mouth opened and out was released a shrieking scream so forceful, that all her limbs shot outwards and stretched her body into a star position. At the peak of her shrieking, the branches of bone that have grown out of her began to vibrate with a furious intensity. Just as she thought her body would snap and crumble into tiny bone fragments, hundreds of feathers emerged from the branches of bone that would now clearly be considered her wings. With her arms, legs, and now wings, fully stretched out, the pain vanished and she remained hovering in the air with her wings flapping grandiose strokes that created low hollowing whooshing sounds. Her eyes opened and it was instantly clear that she would never have greater eyesight than she did at that moment. She could see a fire ant colony building an anthill on the ground, while also being able to analyze the trajectory needed for a flawless flight pattern towards the nearest prey perched hundreds of trees away. Not only was her vision increased, but her peripherals enhanced to the same clarity as to what was right in front of her. She could see both her outstretched hands simultaneously, and made a discovery she was not too pleased to see. Both her hands had turned into more talons and claws than hands and fingers. Her forefinger and middle finger had been cinched together, just as her pinky and ring finger were. Her thumbs were the only things remaining that have been unaltered. Curiously, she glanced at her feet and was not surprised to see that there were no toes there, but talons once again.

"Gives a new meaning to getting your nails done,

huh?" Don said, sending her into a state of surprised shock. Elle had felt his presence near but was unaware of his proximity. Since arriving back into the Waypoint from the previous realm, she had felt closer to him than ever before. She was unsure of the causation or how long it would last, or perhaps if her senses had permanently been altered after going through these doors, but she knew there was a newfound connection between them. She felt tethered to him, not in a restrictive way, but rather in a way that she never had to look too far to find him. He would henceforth always be with her, all she had to do was look internally.

"How long have—"

"The whole damn time!" Don grinned and began to laugh while wiping a tear from the corner of his eye. "The whole time while you were falling, I was right there. I would've damn neared pissed my shorts if I was wearing any." His gear belt was stabilized by being strapped diagonally across his chest. Elle's clothes had also disappeared and her bare breast was exposed. They shrunk and seemed to blend into her torso, but they still had a slight bounce every time she gave her wings a full-fledged flap. The rest of her body was not feathered as fully as her wings were, but did have a short fur-like structure to them. Both their Wrist-Vector had also been altered in size, to be better secured around their thinner limbs.

"It's not funny" Elle flap a single wing at his face and threw him off balance, causing him to somersault in the air. Don quickly regained his positioning without ever skipping a beat with his laughter.

"Okay, okay." He caught his breath. "But you did so well, really." He clapped his hands and as his laughter slowly died off. "Look at you, you're and majestic beauty in this form!"

"Don't try to butter me up." Elle blushed. Buttered up she was indeed, but she knew he meant it. "Are you pleased with yourself?"

"Mayhap."

"Of course, you are. You can't even hide it." She then gave a hearty chuckle herself. Caught her breath and asked, "What if I didn't morph fully in time?"

"Improbable. You're too good at this, a genuine natural."

"So... you want me to stay then?"

"You...I..." He was not ready for such a question. "You know I won't ask that of you, ever." There was no more laughter or lightness to his voice. He lifted his wings far above the center of his head, and with a single powerful swing downward, he flew straight up. He climbed the skies with winged fury. Before putting much thought into action, Elle was right behind him, soaring at top speeds.

The wind felt like a river flowing through the feathers of her wings. She could feel the subtle shifts of the wind, and her wings would automatically adjust to maneuver through the sky. Every minuscule wing adjustment she made, sent her into a completely different flight pattern. She had her vision focused on Don and analyzed every movement of his wings to keep up. "What is the point of this? Just stop flying off!" That was a sentence that came too naturally to her. It still surprised her how quickly not only her body adapted to the changes, but her mind and all of its associations. "Dammit! Stop!" Her voice carried over in a higher pitch than her human voice. It almost squealed, and although he could not hear exactly what she was saying, her message was clear to him. He tucked in his right wing and barreled rolled upwards until he was standing in the sky. Elle soared right up to him and was also hovering upright to look right into his eyes.

"Good to see you can keep up." Don teased.

"Don't change the subject. What is it with you?"

"You already know I won't ask you to stay. It should be just your decision. I don't want to influence you in any way."

"You're kidding, right? I mean what do you think all this is? The doors, the training, the Wrist-Vector. All this because you don't want to influence my decision?"

"That's me just showing you a different perspective. Exposing you to other options you are destined to explore."

"Destiny? Doesn't sound like much of an option then, huh?"

"Elle, you can always choose and make your own decisions. There are always multiple paths in front of you. They all lead generally down the same road, but how you choose to get there is completely up to you. And, I don't want to influence you."

"You mean you don't want me to stay then?" She glanced down. She was only teasing him, but there was some concern on how he might answer. She already was hesitant to allow him too much into her heart. But it was too late for that she supposed.

"I've done this thing alone for so long. Full disclosure, I'm not sure if I can do it any other way, no matter how I feel about you."

"So, we are just going to hover here, staring at each other until you can make up your mind about us? You don't get to make up my mind. You know that, right?"

He looked away and ceased moving his wings for a moment, allowing himself to hear his thoughts better. He returned his glance to meet hers. "But that's what I'm saying. I'm not thinking, and I don't want to think. I just want to show you a part of this life. A part of my life, and in a way, a part of me. If you choose to stay, it will overcome me with joy, but I will not be able to promise you that I won't leave you at some point to continue my mission. And if you choose to go, I will understand since this life is not suited for everyone, and I will miss you dearly. But I will not be able to promise you that I will leave you alone, for what our bond has forged has easily become etched in the echoes of time."

She glided over to him slowly. She placed her morphed hands on his face and with her thumb, caressed his cheek. "That was beautiful, babe. Also, a bit scary, and I'm not really sure what to say except...I also don't want to think about anything else except for existing in this bubble of ours, for as long as possible." She leaned in and kissed him softly. She pressed her lips onto his and had no intention of ever removing them.

He stretched outwards to fully max out his wingspan and curved it forward to encompass Elle and her wings. He gently used his wings to pull her in and wrap her completely into his arms. With both of their wings wrapped around one another, they began to drift downwards. As they began to fall towards the ground, their kiss became fueled with passion.

The more they fell, the more they kissed.

The faster they fell, the faster they kissed.

Being wrapped within his wings, she was unaware of the rate they were falling at, but she felt safe. He was always very protective of her, and it made her feel completely safe. It wasn't until he adjusted his wings to compensate for the wind being uprooted beneath them, that she realized truly just how fast they were falling. She gasped and jolted backward a bit, ready to bail and fly away to save her life, but he grabbed her by the shoulders and gripped tight. "I got you," he whispered while looking into her eyes. "I got you." She sank back into his arms, allowing his wings to encircle her once again. "Do you want me to let go?"

"No." She began to kiss his neck and while leaving tiny bite marks, made a trail up to his ear. "I want..." she gave more kisses, more tiny bites, "...you to" she kissed his ear and pulled on his earlobe, "...to be" more kisses, more tiny bites, "inside of me." She continued to kiss and bite his neck to stimulate him more, but he was already rock hard. She pressed her body close to him and could feel the smooth curvature of the tip of his dick rub against her clitoris. She squirmed and teased him, and he squirmed and teased her back. Don then for the quickest of moments released his grip on her completely, and she shot downward and felt his cock shoot upward into her. She gasped and held her breath as he quickly grabbed her shoulders once again. His talons dug into her more this time, as he used his hold on her to balance and gain proper momentum to best fuck her. Their bodies twirled and rolled in the air, but within the capsule of sex created by wrapped wings, there was nothing much else that mattered. As his grip increased, his talons pierced the skin of her shoulders, and a tiny amount of blood winked out of the pinched skin. It grew and began to pool, but as soon as any small amount accumulated, it was taken by the wind and flew upward into the sky. They had stopped kissing each other at this point and were only looking into each other's eyes. Their pupils dilated as they looked deep into each other, and Don continued to be deep in her. Their mutual ecstasy was not only felt but each wince and twitch of the pupil was seen. He then reached down and grabbed one leg at a time, before throwing them above his shoulders.

With her ankles by his ears and her knees pressed on her breast, he pounded her with no resistance in-between their blissful existence.

She moaned, he grunted. They made beautiful sounds uninterrupted.

As she still bled from her shoulders, familiar tension began to build inside of her. Her breath escaped her, and also remained trapped within her lungs. She quickly wrapped her arms around his back and clawed at it. She arched her back while digging in his. The red striations caused by her talons ripping on his back quickly turned into battle wounds. Blood that once belonged inside of him, now flew out, up into the sky, joining the blood escaping Elle's shoulders. Their bodies continued to plummet towards the ground as he continued to pummel her pussy. Behind them, was a stream of their combined blood that left a trail of proof of their vigorous lovemaking.

They looked like a comet falling from the sky to anyone glancing at them from off in the distance. A comet that was nearing the floor below. Neither of the two participants of this sex comet knew how dangerously close they were truly getting the ground below.

Pain and pleasure mixed an intoxicating cocktail that began to stir an immense orgasm inside of her. "Yes," she began to whimper. "More." Tiny waves of electricity began to roll through her and ripple throughout. His grip on her tightened. Her talons found their way to his lower back where she dug them in to find their new home. She squeezed and his butt flexed and pumped full thrusts harder into her. Her cheeks became flushed with heat, and her lower core ignited. She began to cum inside and out, numbing her body and making her lightheaded. An aftermath of shudders wrecked her body in phases, sending her orgasm to every known nerve cell of her body. She squeezed and twitched shivering pleasures until melting into his arms.

He held her close and kissed her as her convulsions dimmed into a heavy, melting body. It was, only then that Don realized he was now the only one that would stop their plummet into the ground. He glanced below them to see that there was only a mere 20 feet left before they would become splatter cake. He quickly unwrapped his wings and swung Elle onto her back to carry her just as newlyweds do, one hand under the knees and the other across her back. He landed on the ground by simultaneously squatting down with his knees and propelling downwards with his wings. His technique absorbed the landing effectively, and he was able to gently lay Elle down. He curled up next to her and spooned her. He wrapped his arm and wing over her and pulled her close. They laid there, silently and peacefully.

Calm. Calmness. Hearts beating and lungs breathing. Calmness. Calm.

CHAPTER 23

Their enlarged ribcages took slow and deep breathes. Don was unsure of how long they had laid there, but a small sample of curiosity began to disturb his thoughts. The last he remembered, the Sun was setting back at the Waypoint, and he had not set a reminder on his Wrist-Vector. He doubted that they were near Door crawling time, but he also doubted his doubt.

"Hey," he gently nudged her in case she was asleep.

"Hey." Judging by the sound of it, she was just in that phase before drifting off.

"Did you by chance set an alarm? You know, for when the Doors begin to crawl?"

"Umm, no..." She sat up and turned to face him. "Shit, I'm sorry."

"No. No, not at all. It's not on you."

"Don't treat me like some rookie, I know when I messed up."

"Seriously, I barely even told you what type of realm this was. You adapted proficiently and I couldn't be prouder."

Elle smiled, blew him a kiss in the air, and stood up. "Thanks. Let's just go, just in case."

Don was in full agreement. He lifted himself off the

ground completely and began to fly above the treetops. Elle was directly to his left and soaring just a wingspan away. They soared through the air with grace as the wind guided them back towards the door. He glanced at her, stunned by not only her beauty but by her level of aptitude. She had consistently proven herself to not only be an excellent student but a force to be reckoned with. Don's competitive nature began to stir him up. He felt the urge to compete, unlike he had in a long time. He locked eyes with her and stuck his tongue out in a jovial and mocking way. He shot a glance to the path in front of them with a suggestive nod, and then right back to her. She smirked. She flashed him a wink, flapped her wings fiercely, and took off.

The gust she left behind ruffled his feathered arms and threw him slightly off balance. He expected her to agree to a race, but he did not expect her to be so quick in her start. He frowned at being bested at the start of the race, then chuckled at the thought of how much fun he was having, just by simply being in a race. Something he hasn't done in years, but for some reason felt compelled to do so now and to do so with her. He angled his wings upwards and began to climb the skies while pressing forward. Elle was gaining distance from him as he was swinging his wings with intense effort.

The tendons that lead from under his armpit to the extended bone structure that made up his wings were being stretched to their utmost limit. The muscles next to them started to build Latic acid and began to create a burning sensation. His breathing became labored but found a pattern and he focused on it. He let all other thoughts breeze by him. The door was now visible, and his flight path became clear. He tilted his wings, and with the assistance of the downward momentum he was now receiving, he gained incredible speed. The pain began to transition into euphoria and his face began to tingle. The rhythm of his wings flapping turned into a methodical and focused tempo. The wind in his ears drowned out his worries, concerns, and distorted time itself. He was in a groove, and an endorphin-fueled rush swept over him.

He was making impeccable time and caught up to her quickly. The door was a mere half a dragon's breath away and he dove headfirst relentlessly. He swooped from above her and dove headfirst into the door. He passed through, and with the remaining momentum, morphed back into his normal body and rolled out of the doorway. His body thumped the ground underneath, raising loose soil into the air and filling his face with dirt. He ended his roll sprawled out on the ground, panting for air as his lungs readjusted to their normal-sized ribcage. A few moments later and Elle appeared, her normal self, breathing just fine. She walked over to him and looked down, "You won, sure, but you look like a hot mess."

"All I heard was 'you win', so whatever else you said doesn't count." A quick grin followed by him sticking out his tongue was how he chose to respond to her. Amused, but visibly upset, she fake-kicked him on his legs. He laughed as her competitive side was clearly showing. "You're too cute."

She stopped with the kicks and glared at him for a moment before she gazed off into the distance. He did not think that what he said was in any way inappropriate, but he still examined her eyes and face for any signs of micro expressions that may have indicated her thoughts. "You know what, you won, but only that round!" She sprinted off. Her arms swinging full force and straight down the hill.

"No!" A very clear and loud shout roared out of his mouth.

"I'll win this next one." She leaned her body forward and pumped her arms harder. She was dashing past doors. She glanced back to gauge the distance she had created but made sure not to slow her pace. He was running as fast as he could. She knew it was only a matter of time before he caught up to her. She decided this was the most opportune moment to enter another door. She ran up to the nearest door around, grabbed the doorknob, and passed through with no hesitation. In her haste, she forgot to check the door for any markings. Had she looked, she would have seen that there were no markings on the door indicating what may lay beyond. This door...had never been opened before by Don, or by any of his friends.

CHAPTER 24

Unlike the other doors she had passed through that day, the vibration that usually consumed her body during her morph was not present. She presumed it was because she had started to become much more efficient at it, and her transformation was already complete. She looked around to see what kind of new atmosphere she was in, but could only see shades of grey clouding her entire field of view. She figured perhaps her eyes were going to take a little longer to adjust to this new environment. The next best thing she considered was to conduct a visual scan of herself, for that might have given way to a clue of what type of world she was now a part of. She looked down but saw nothing except that same grey and cloudy matter as before. She immediately raised the palms of her hands to meet her at eye level, yet when she looked, she noticed nothing different. She looked left, looked right, and was surrounded by it. She thought there was a slim chance that perhaps, she just never opened her eyes at all, so she felt her face for her eyes. She made sure to take her time and feel for her eyelashes and pulled her eyelids apart slowly. Her eyes were definitely open, but there was nothing to see.

She started to become concerned with her situation.

She wanted to take a few steps, maybe walk out of this haze, but she could not feel her feet. Her concern grew into worry. Her worry laid the path for fear to enter. She was mentally telling herself to walk forward but could not feel if she was at all. She reached down to feel for her legs and began to notice that her hands were also not making contact with anything. There was no sense of direction and her senses were failing her. She inhaled through her nose and took a deep breath in. She could feel her lungs take in air, but could smell nothing, nor taste anything. Her hands and feet appeared to be numb and she frantically began to pat herself all over her body. It felt as if she was wearing a few layers of gloves, and with each passing sweep, she felt less and less. She opened her mouth and tried to shout for anyone. She knew she was recently with someone, or perhaps it was a group of people...or maybe it was just her this entire time, all alone. All alone, all along. Her shouts produced no sound or at least no sound that she could hear. All her senses were nullified until it seemed that she had none at all. All alone, all along. This phrase was now one of the very few, and only thoughts she would have. She once again began to look around, but this time, she was no longer looking for anything, nor anyone. She was simply observing the grey emptiness around her, and her mind was becoming as clouded as her surroundings. She remembered for a brief moment that she was supposed to be doing something or going somewhere, but that was all she could recollect.

All alone, all along.

Yes, this empty feeling was now starting to make more sense than the empty searching. She felt comfort in knowing she had always been alone, and that it has been like that all along. She did not know, however, why she felt so sad and why she wanted to cry...it didn't matter though, because she didn't how to. She was no longer able to recognize herself as a participant of the human race.

Her essence was dissipating.

All alone, all along.

Her mind was deteriorating.

She was no longer she; she had become simply an...it, and it was consumed, and it was alone...all along.

CHAPTER 25

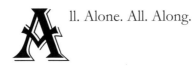 ll. Alone. All. Along.

CHAPTER26

All. Alone.

CHAPTER 27

All Along

CHAPTER 28

All …

CHAPTER 29

CHAPTER 30

Don witnessed her pass through the door and his immediate concern was the time of day. He glanced at the horizon which was now dusted by darkness and knew it wouldn't be much longer before the doors began to crawl. He set his Wrist-Vector to alarm him when it was time to go. He set a 20 minutes buffer time, and then another for when there were only 5 minutes left. He had never once heard the 5 minutes alarm go off, but it was a habit he kept to ensure the urgency of safety. He knew that once he passed through the door, there would not be enough time to explore. He had to find Elle and talk her into returning as soon as possible. With Chris gone, there would be nobody left to search for them or to even know that they were lost in space and time.

He approached the door and just as soon as he began to turn the doorknob, he released it in horror. He was ready to enter the doorway knowing that she would not have crossed without looking for the notch indicator on the door. Yet here he was, standing before a door with no notches. He bent over and got as close as possible to visually inspect the door for any notch indicator. Even the smallest of etchings would have provided some comfort. None was found. The door had been fully intact without a grain disturbed. He supposed it was better than going through a doorway with an X marking. As for taunting as it was, there was still hope that what laid beyond that door was a positive and habitable realm. If it was not, then he had to locate Elle as soon as possible and hope that she was able to manage on her own. He took a deep breath and walked through.

As the vibrations that passed his body settled, and his vision focused, he was able to see that he was in front of a large warehouse. Immediately after walking into the vast space, he looked forward, and out appeared a large pipe, that was directly in front of him. It looked like any other pipe he had ever seen, except it was moving fast, and moving directly towards him. Directly towards his face, he noticed. Before he was able to react to it, the side of the pipe fiercely connected with the side of his face, and rendered him unconscious. His body stiffened for a moment as his eyes rolled backward, and then immediately collapsed to the floor.

Don would remain unconscious and would never find out exactly for how long, for when his consciousness did return, and the slightest amount of mental cognition occurred, it was immediately apparent to him that he was fucked. He was an upside-down cake in a blender fucked and probably would be for a long time.

His right eye opened faster than his left, primarily due to the swelling accrued from the pipe attack, but also due to the bright light emanating from a desk lamp next to him. The lampshade was removed, and the neck of the lamp was bent so that the bulb shined directly onto his bruised face. Once both eyes were able to fully open, he realized that he was upright and sitting, and that was the only positive part of his situation. His hands and elbows were tied up with rope behind the chair, and of course, so were his feet. His cloudy mind leaned towards denial of this entire situation, but he quickly realized it was best to settle into this present moment before he became too overwhelmed. He instinctively attempted to wriggle his arms free, but before expending too much energy on this useless task, he settled once again. He took a visual report of his surroundings and the first thing he saw was a male figure standing before him. There stood a man of average height, with a below-average body fat percentage. It was not that he was muscular or fit in any sort of way, but rather in an unhealthy and starving type of condition. He had dirty clothes that matched his dirty long hair. His face was thin and weary, yet the anger in his eyes filled his aurora and distracted him from any other feature being more pronounced. He was staring directly into Don's eyes, and with every moment passing, it was noticeable that he was more and more displeased with his presence.

Don was still light-headed and could feel his eyes roll around in their socket from time to time. He did the only thing he knew how to regain some clarity and control of his body. He took deep and elongated breathes to flood his system with oxygen and slow his resting heart rate.

"No...Use...Seeker." The pipe wielder slithered his words into the air and they fell harshly into Don's head. One never knows what to expect when hearing someone's voice for the first time, but Don knew that this voice belonged to someone who hasn't used his vocal cords in a long time. The voice cracked as it was forcefully spoken. The elongated syllables created an even wider distorted sound. The man speaking these words, however, never flinched or grimaced as he glared directly into Don's pupils. "You and your...methods, have no power here."

Don, confused about who this individual was, became irrationally enraged by his tone and words. He made a serious attempt to rip himself free from bondage. He ignored the pain the rope inflicted on his wrists and tried again. All he managed to accomplish was a strained shoulder muscle. This unknown figure keeled over and laughed at this spectacle, and his laughter was worse than his voice. It sounded more like an attempt to catch air than a joyous reaction. It was rough and produce phlegm that sputtered out his mouth.

It was then that Don saw what was directly behind this disgusting thing of a person, and it made him freeze in place. He slowed down his breathwork so he could focus and observe all the details. More denial entered his mind, but there was too much visual certainty and emotional attachment to what he was witnessing for it to be a hoax. Elle laid horizontally, floating in the air behind him. She was surrounded by a dark grey cloud that moved in a clockwise and fluid motion around her. It swirled around her like a dreadful mist that wanted to consume her for supper. The dark cloud was at its darkest around her head, making it difficult to confirm her level of consciousness, but as he peered into it, he could see her chest slowly rise and fall. Angered, confused, and now worried, Don has lost track of his emotions and his mind became foggy as well.

The dark muddy cloud around Elle started to become transparent and thin out. The numerous swirls of grey matter almost appeared to turn into still dust particles floating alongside her. The choking laughter of the grotesque male-ended abruptly and he turned to face Elle. "You see her...and now, I will continue to make her see nothing." He raised his hands, closed his eyes, mumbled some jargon he never heard before, and witnessed the cloud around her once again grow opaque and thicken. Don watched him continue to speak unknown words and push his palms towards her. The words hasten in tempo and the swirl sped up in conjunction. This dark cloud had now morphed into a full eggshell around her, and her body was barely visible.

"Stop it! Cease your sorcery at once!" These words raced out of his mouth and as distance in dialect as they sounded to Don, it felt natural to him. He was letting many things consume him, his focus was fleeting but his instincts seemed to be taking over. He pressed his toes into the ground and attempted to hop towards them. His unfocused mind seemed to not make enough of a connection to his body because his body wanted to go, but the ropes tying him down prevented all that. His chair scooted not more than a mere centimeter, and once again, the figure began to cackle in amusement.

"I am Tuloki, and I am no sorcerer you fool. Do you not recognize one of your own?" He reached behind his back and revealed an Ahir Blade. He flipped the blade into the air and he spread out his palm as if to catch it, but instead, it levitated a few inches above his hand. It too was surrounded by the same style of smoke that encompassed Elle's body.

"You lie. You are no Realm Seeker, and that isn't your blade. Let it go...and let her go!"

"You sound like a child. Do you really think your empty demands will persuade me to do anything you say?" Tuloki tapped his finger onto the tip of the blade and it began to rotate on its own until it was pointed at Don's face. "And like this blade, this Nomad is mine. You would best remember that before this blade becomes the last thing you ever taste."

"And do you really think I will believe any of your lies?" Don's hands were tied behind his back, but luckily, it was right around where his own Ahir Blade would be stowed on his gear belt. With the little movement he did have, he wriggled his hands and reached with his fingers in an attempt to locate it.

Tuloki sighed and gave a short chuckle. "I must say,

Don, I'm going to get exhausted laughing at you." Tuloki cupped his other hand, began to rotate his wrist and from behind his back came levitating out another Ahir Blade being propelled by the dark grey mist.

Don was once again in such awe and confusion that his breathing became stagnant. It was not witnessing his own blade being taunted in front of him, nor was it the eerie magic that seemed to easily flow through this person before him that placed him at such unease. What truly was occupying his tormented brain, was that this person in front of him had spoken his name. His mind began to construct the few possible ways that he could have come across this information, and each scenario grew bleaker and produce worry upon his facial expression. With the certainty that Don knew this man could not be trusted, he still asked his most pressing question. "How... how do you know my name?"

The exasperated expression presented on Tuloki's face slowly twisted into one of amusement. "Oh, I don't know your name. But this Nomad does. I've infiltrated her mind the moment she passed through the door and learned everything I needed. That's how I know your insignificant name, and that's how I knew you were going to come flying through that door looking for her so desperately. By now, she is lost in the void of her mind, or perhaps it's already just gone too far. No way to tell, but that won't matter. I have no intentions of bringing her back. She'll just rot away on the ground once I leave, as you too will helplessly rot away in that chair."

"Why are you doing this to her, and to me? What do you have to gain? Just work with me and I'm sure with my resources I'll be able to get you what you need."

"Need?" Tuloki clenched his fist and the two blades jetted forward towards Don's face while leaving a thin trail of dark smoke behind them. They sliced through the air without any signs of slowing down. They reached within inches of his eyeballs before coming to a jolting stop. Don could sense the exaggerating in his voice before even considering that the blades would ever reach that close to him, so he didn't flinch. This only upset Tuloki even more. "What I needed was not to be left alone here to fucking die! What I needed, was for the rest of my team to come to get me out of this shithole so I didn't need to scrape off the thin carcasses of whatever meat I could find in these wastelands. You fucking Seekers are a joke and all full of shit! Valeria is a sham and I intend on exposing them. Then, as they scramble to piece together damage control, I intend on destroying them and burning it all down."

"Why are you telling me all this? It's way too much information for me to think you're being credible." Don knew that all of his facial micro-expressions were being analyzed, so he tried to be as stoic as possible. "Sounds like, you're trying to convince me as much as you are trying to convince yourself."

"Your words are a false as your face, Seeker. I told you already, I know everything you know, plus a whole other set of dimensional powers that they don't teach you." Tuloki sucked his teeth and shrugged his shoulders. "I guess the pleasure I find in destroying your reality, brings me as much pleasure as the harm I'm about to inflict on your lover here" He finished his sentence with a sly grin.

Don hoped that his stern display of not being phased by the blades would bother Tuloki to the point where it would cause him to make himself vulnerable. Yet, it seemed that his act was transparent. Although Tuloki had not made himself vulnerable, he did expose a lot of information, and from Don's experience, sometimes information is the most powerful weapon someone could wield. He would continue in his attempt to extrapolate as much information as he possibly could. "If you are truly a Realm Seeker, then why would you want to destroy the very element that made you who you are?"

"Don't question me. Just witness me." Tuloki waved his hands and the blades followed. They glided along the nearest wall, and when they reached a rusty juncture, they remained hovering. The wall separated along the rusted section and slowly creaked upwards to reveal a hidden cabinet. On display were at least a half dozen more Ahir Blades, all lined up in a row. Underneath them followed a row of Wrist-Vectors, some broken, and some like new, but all very much authentic. There was no confusing these with cheap knock-offs, which meant that there was also no way for Don to be in denial that their previous owners were most likely dead. Tuloki sent Don's Ahir Blade into the cabinet and sent the other back into his backside where its sheath remained.

"You're not the first fool to think they would have another ending to their story, only to be interrupted by my mission, and wind-up dead by my hands. The difference with you, however, is that you are the only idiot to bring a Nomad into these parts. Fortunately for you, this means you still may live a while longer. The only reason you're not dead and I have allowed you to continue breathing is because I need one piece of easily-given information from you. These other seekers decided they would much rather die than give it up. You, however, I can quite literally taste your devotion to this floating soon-to-be corpse next to me. You want her to live? Then tell me, what are the current coordinates of the (main location)? Simple. So simple really." Tuloki raised both his hand and shrugged again, "Whatdya say, pal?"

Once the wall opened and its contents displayed, Don was fixated and never looked away. He began to realize that this maniac was never really stuck here, he had the opportunity to step through the door before but had chosen to remain here. Chosen to suffer an unknown amount of time until he found someone who would give him these coordinates. Of course, Don believed that he wasn't going to tell him anything tangible, but Tuloki felt that he might. He knew he had to use that to his tactical advantage somehow, and without placing Elle at risk. Little pieces of the puzzle began to come together about this whole situation, but not nearly enough for him to formulate any type of strategic plan. Most importantly, he still didn't know what type of magic he was against, nor how he knew so much about Realm Seekers. Don had read about the use of dark magic before, but this was not something that was commonly seen or even spoken about. Many of his peers never displayed any intentions of seeking out this dark information, especially after completing theValeria Academy. Most were just grateful to be a part of something so spectacular, so to question anything else was unheard of.

"I don't want you to hurt her, you understand?"

"Then tell me what I want to know."

"You want me to give up every I vowed to protect, but for what? Sure, you're upset and blah, blah and what not. But why? I need to know."

"You vowed to protect an organization that has been lying to you, and to everyone else in the universe, that's why. You should focus more on your vow to protect her before it's too late and her mind is lost forever."

Don lowered his head and his voice. He needed to make him believe that he was being convinced, but slowly and with hesitation. "Yeah, I can't say I've always been too akin to their message of all peace for all time, but that doesn't mean I want to put all those people in danger."

"Don't woooorry" Tuloki ears perked up at hearing

that Don was being convinced. He stepped closer to him. "I'm only after the council, all others can go disappear for all I care." He crouched down and was now at eye level with Don. "They left me here you know...to die. I was on their most forefront squad, mapping the universe and whatnot. For years I was putting up the numbers of new realms and creating treaties with other worlds on behalf of the Valeria. But as soon as the storms began to occur more frequently in Joshua Hills, they decided to reroute my squad and send us back to peace-keeping missions. Do I look like a bleak peacekeeper? Fuck that, I told them. I stayed right here and began to teach myself. And look at all that I've learned." He placed his palms on the ground and the earth began to vibrate. Pebbles and stones began to levitate from the ground. "I can feel the energy of this planet and am feeding of it, and can crack this planet in half if I wanted to!" His pupils grew in diameter and the white sclera in his eyes turn dark and cloudy. "All this they hid from us, Don. All this power they want to keep for themselves! For that, they must be vanquished, and a new society created." He blinked rapidly and the color of his eyes returned. He lifted his hand off the ground and softened his voice. "You see, you can't trust them, and all that they have hidden from us."

Don was now actually uncomfortable, and he did not know how much to believe from him. Yet, what he saw and felt was undeniable. The ground shook not only his body but his core and belief system. Ultimately what he decided was that Tuloki was still too dangerous to trust, Elle was still in danger, and time was passing by closer and closer to the doors crawling.

Don tried to appear as sheepish as possible. "So, you just want the coordinates, and then you will release her from your spell, and then leave us here?"

"Yeeess." His subtle excitement slithered through his teeth. "Give me the exact coordinates now, and yes, you two will be just fine." Don saw this as his only opportunity to use his Wrist-Vector to call for reinforcements and distract him long enough for them to arrive.

"I don't have it memorized, but I'll pull it up. I need my hands, of course. And maybe some reassurance by placing her on the ground would really go a long way in easing my nerves, you know?" Tuloki did not look persuaded to follow any of his requests. He remained there staring at him and analyzing his every micro-expression again. Like two still portraits they existed in each other's visual field until finally Tuloki winked at him and gave him a half-smile. He then took a few paces towards where Elle was suspended mid-air and spoke a few words in a whisper, and in a tongue unfamiliar to Don. Her body lowered to the ground but the dark shadows around her grew thicker and darker.

"Lowered, but with increased protection. I don't like you, nor do I trust you, but I certainly don't fear you either. Now go, give me the coordinates." Tuloki snapped his fingers and a black spark jumped from his fingertips and landed on the rope that bound his hands. A maroon ember emerged and slowly disintegrated the rope fibers.

Since being tied to the chair, Don had received so much information and at a constant rate. He barely thought about how he was bound and incapable of normal movement. It was typical for him in these types of situations to remain still and become very observant, but when those ropes slid off him, he was surprised to feel the amount of relief that washed over him. His muscles twitched from being used after a long period of hiatus, and even though he wanted to stretch them out, he knew he had little time to organize a distress call before Tuloki demanded a set of coordinates. Being that his elbows were still bound, he had to use much of his energy to twist his torso and stretch his arms to where his Wrist-Vector and hands were just barely visible in his peripheral vision.

He began to turn the dial and adjust the crystal into position. Locking into the appropriate wavelength that connected him back to Valeria always took some time, but he never really noticed exactly how long until now. Until every second counted. The crystal rotated itself and teetered slightly as his location was being honed in on. Don didn't know exactly where he was so he couldn't manually insert his location, which only prolonged the process. All he could do was sit there and wait until a signal could be resonated and locked.

Tuloki's eyes narrowed. "FUCKING STOP!" His hands raised above his head and swirls of deep black smoke emanated from his palms. With a swift swoop down past his hips, his hands pushed the smoke outward and they wrapped around Don's hands. The speed of the smoke forced them behind his back and once again, and he was once again bound and immobilized. The smoke produced no heat but they stung and burned his wrists. Although they were not as tight as the ropes, he would have much rather preferred them than the painful stings produced by the rotating smoke. The pain was a constant barrage of hot pins and electric needles that seem to cut into his skin. "Do you think me a fool? Honestly?" While cursing under his breath he approached Don who was poorly attempting his best not to flinch at the pain in his wrist. He didn't have to raise his hand too far when he grabbed the neck of his sitting victim. "I want coordinates. Ones you can instantly bring up! There is no need for you to wait for jack shit unless you were trying to backstab me." Tuloki squeezed his Adam's apple until he was audibly wheezing. He gripped just tight enough where it was making him extremely unpleasant and difficult to breathe, but not enough to where he would pass out. "Take a free note, wait until you have my back if you to backstab me."

Without relinquishing his grip, he stomped on the ground with demonic fury. Seams and trails of dark energy began to radiate off his skin and form around him. With his free hand, he reached over to the bent lamp that was positioned right next to them and palmed the back of it. With all of his anger being manifested into the dark matter encircling his arms, he swung both hands towards each other with the intent of creating a large thunderous clap. The only adjustment was that in between his hands was the exposed lightbulb, and Don's face. The two subjects met each other like two trains crashing at full speed. Shards of glass were embedded into the side of his face, and blood splattered down the neck of the lamp. There was no evidence of a lightbulb ever being installed, since every piece of it was now either on the ground, or had found a new home in his skin.

Tuloki dropped the lamp and was visibly heaving in frustration, but with some content. His teeth rattled as he took a deep breath to where his ribcage expanded quite visibly. He then brought his face to meet Don directly at eye level. "I have no time for this. I will not be here when the doors begin to crawl...you will die. How slowly that comes to be, is now the only variable that is allotted to you!" He squeezed his neck to the point where Don was certain that the cartilage would snap and he would swallow it in bits. His windpipe was narrowed to where only a whistle passed through. He began to see small black dots sparkle in his vision and became light-headed. "You will not die until I get those coordinates, Seeker." He released his grip and walked away.

Don immediately gasped for air, but then winced in agonizing pain. The rush of air felt like swallowing lava. The oxygen that flowed into his body brought some clarity into his vision but the pain produced tears. Short flashes of gasps were all that he could produce, to only be interrupted by a burst of coughs. As he struggled to gain any sort of control over his life, Tuloki walked past Elle and began to rummage around in a desk by the opposite wall. He grabbed a few tools that were not discernable from Don's view; partially due to proximity, but mostly the tears that still filled his eyes.

"I'm not going to ask you again. I'm going to be very busy now so please don't interrupt. Unless you have the coordinates." He placed all his tools behind the chair, to ensure that Don could not see and prepare mentally for what he was about to do to him. He was familiar with the meditation practices they taught at Valeria since, after all, he was also a graduate of their program. Knowing what is about to come could greatly aid one in preparing for it mentally, and therefore able to combat its effect. He knew he did not have time to spar with Don in the art of mental combat. Only physical torture was what remained, and that was an art form that he had been perfecting since his team left him behind.

He grabbed a pincer plier and gently clamped Don's right pinky finger. He applied pressure until he broke skin and blood appeared. Don kept quiet. He knew this was only the beginning and could not show weakness so soon. It would not be credible, and would only thwart his actual plan. He intended of displaying a gradual deterioration of physical tolerance to whatever happened to him. Hopefully, faking most of the pain at a later point, and ultimately leading to Tuloki lowering his guard once more.

"This little piggy went wee, wee—" The pliers clamped down harder now, crunching the small bone between its teeth, "—rip!" A chunk of his pinky finger departed from its hand, and an audible grunt fell from Don's mouth. He quickly began to reassess his original plan. There would be no gradual pain scale here. The doors would crawl soon, and Don was now certain that Tuloki had full intention of making it back by then.

The pliers found their way to his ring finger next. With no taunting chant or inclination of hesitation, Tuloki ripped the tip of his ring finger clean off. "Shit!" Don was not faking anything now, and he was only a minute into this torture.

"Oh boy, that little piggy sure was eager to go!" A laugh creaked out of Tuloki's grinning teeth. Don could not see it but could feel his daunting breath near the back of his head from his wide-open mouth. "Take this." Tuloki laid a piece of blank paper on his lap. "I want numbers on this." Blood smeared by where he was gripping the page. "Actually, You. You want numbers on this page. The sooner I get them, the sooner this all ends." With the tip of the finger still attached to the pliers, Tuloki took it and tapped him with the fingertip on the side of his head. "Think Don, think." With a few more taps from his bloody fingertip, Don could hear another laugh begin to arise. "This." Tap, tap. "Could all." Tap, tap. "End." The tapping finger went from the side of his skull and began to slide along his cheekbone. "Now, I know what you're thinking, bud." Don could smell his blood as the finger slide across his nose and onto his lips. "But I need you not to think. Just Shhhhh." Tuloki pressed the finger firmly onto Don's lips, to the point where it was resting on his teeth, and he could taste his blood. Tuloki grinned and a single eyebrow raised. "Are you ready to tell me?"

Don creaked his neck forward and bit onto his separated finger, and ripped it from the grasp of the pliers. He turned his head and spit it out with force. "Go fuck yourself!"

"Okay...I see." Tuloki was unphased and even smirked

REALMS OF LUST AND LOVE

a little. He moved the plier to the next finger. Instead of gripping the entire middle finger, he slid one side of the pliers deep into and under the nail. This alone jolted pain directly into Don's spine, causing him to have his lips pressed together in order not to yelp.

Only once the plier reached halfway into his nailbed, Tuloki clamped the teeth down and secured a tight grip, and spoke out loud. "That paper will either save you or hurt you. Are you ready to write down the coordinates?" Once, again, Don did not budge or make any indication of the level of pain he was experiencing. Then with one hand on Don's hand and the other gripping tightly onto the pliers, he yanked as hard as he could, ripping the entire nail off his finger. This sent Don into an immediate convulsion of pain.

He twitched and bucked on his chair. His eyes shot open and bulged, his shoulders stiffened, and began to cramp. His hands were bloody and bound. Blood oozed down his three outer fingers as the dark smoke continued to circulate his wrists. The binding mist still inflicted continuous sharp and electrical pain, but with his nail being recently ripped out, his right hand fell momentarily numb. He tried wiggling his fingers to regain sensation but was met nothing.

Better numb hands than pain-filled ones he thought. His shoulders released their tightness and his eyes relaxed once again. His vision fell upon Elle. He could barely see her through the dark shell that encompassed her body. He felt envy for a moment that she was just lying there, but he knew that he was the only one that could save the both of them now. He had to regain his focus, but all he could think about was how distant he felt from her. She was within his vision, yet miles away from being able to hold her again. He debated the possibility of ever holding her again, and the calculations were not in his favor. Don realized that he was quickly losing focus, and his thoughts were beginning to roam wild. He had to step up, he had to.

CHAPTER 31

O nly seconds had passed since his nail was ripped out of his right hand, yet his thoughts had shoved a months' worth of worry and doubt into himself. He had forgotten all about his current situation and was lost in the fear of the future. Of the potential lack of future to be accurate. This time it wasn't himself to snap him back into the present, but rather the sensation of him regaining feeling in his hand. His fingers throbbed in isolation. Agony shifted from his mind back into his body.

"Since you won't be using this, I figure you won't mind if I borrow it for a little, right," Tuloki said matter-of-factly as he reached over and grabbed the piece of paper from his lap. He folded a standard 8 ½ x 11 paper in half. With one hand he pressed Don's fingers against his own back, and with the other, he grabbed the paper along the folded edge. He brought the paper and lined it up over the exposed skin from the ripped fingernail. In a smooth and fierce motion, he pressed the edge of the paper into the soft skin by his nailbed and slide it fast. He slid the paper off him so fast that at first, it appeared that no damage was done. Then, two razor-thin lines of darker blood arose from the already bloody skinned finger. These razor-sharp papercuts sent Don immediately back into a convulsion of horrific pain. This time his eyes slammed shut and his teeth grinded from how hard he was clenching his jaw. He felt like his entire finger was just sliced off. Don had not felt physical pain like this in a long time. To imagine that such a paramount pain came from such a small and minor event, made him question his ability to focus and overcome what was yet to come. Don wanted to scream but he had yet begun breathing. Either he was incapable or simply forgot, but after his initial gasp of air, his diaphragm stiffened, along with the rest of his body. His body went from seizing with pain to a steady tremor that would not ease up. It was the only thing that Don noticed from being overwhelmed with painful sensory input. He took that as his first step into regulating his body. He finally took a breath and felt accomplished at just doing that.

He continued to breathe steady, and hard while bringing the rest of his focus in on the pain. This was the only thing he could control now. He had to focus to better process all the pain and remove himself from spiraling out. He focused and tried to imagine the exact location on his nail bed that was sliced open. He imagined all the ruptured cells and atoms that were involved in producing this pain. He concentrated the pain to just that area, which seemed to make the rest of his body self-regulate.

Tuloki sucked his teeth. "It is a shame you missed out on your one chance to live. Honestly, I didn't even need you. All I need is a Wrist-Vector to get out from here, ergo why your friend is laying in the void over there. But once I saw her mind, and that you were coming in, well that was just a bonus. I kept you alive so you could expedite my plan in locating those liars. But a fresh Wrist-Vector with blood still pumping through its owner's arm long enough for me to pass through the door is enough for me to finally move on from here. You are quickly becoming more of a worthless bother. Yet still, I don't mind seeing you crumble under my hands. It is quite satisfying for now...and once it's not, and there are no coordinates on that paper, well then, I guess our time will be up and it'll be your turn to rot away." Tuloki grabbed his other hand now and gripped the pliers once again.

Don had heard most of what he said. There was still faint disorientation that he was fighting through, but he mustered what energy he could and spoke. "Time."

"Errm...What?"

"You said—" Don inhaled a painful breath, "—time. That our time will be up." He took a deeper breath and raised his head to look at him. "Our time is already up; the doors are about to crawl." As he finished those words, his Wrist-Vector activated its first alarm signaling they had but 20 minutes before the door closed on them for good.

"Son-uva-bitch!" Tuloki sucked his teeth again. He was surprised by Don's accuracy, but even more surprised that his plan had to be abruptly hastened when he was prepared to continue his experiments on him. He wanted those coordinates, regardless of whatever facade he placed on display. "Fine. This carnival will end. But you're going to see what happens next. I'm going to make sure it is burned into your memory, you fuck!" Tuloki threw the metal pliers like a baseball at Don's face. With there being no moment for anticipation of his throw, the metal tool struck Don directly on the bridge of his nose, sending an immediate gush of bright red blood down both nostrils. With tears filling up his eyes from the reaction of the impact, blood dripping down the back of his throat and face, it was impossible to see where Tuloki had gone off to. Don was interchanging swallowing what felt like pints of copper fluid, and blinking his eyes rapidly so he could see again, Tuloki reappeared and slapped his palm on top of Don's scalp.

"You are going to see what I do to your Nomad girlfriend, and then I'll leave you here, incapable to ever see another image again. Your eyeballs will be my lil' souvenir of this most tedious exchange." Tuloki slid his palm down his forehead. and slammed it back onto the headrest of the chair. He pinched his left eyelid by the lashes and pulled them until they stretched out as far as possible. With his other hand, he raised a single hole puncher in front of the stretched eyelid, and meticulously slide it in. Once the hole puncher was centered on the eyelid, he clamped down and produced a 2mm hole on his eyelid. He lifted the hole puncher and a tab of skin flopped onto the ground below. Tuloki decided it was still not large enough and repeated this procedure two more times on the same eyelid. A triad of oblong circle holes was left on the eyelid of the now screaming owner. Don railed his screams so loud it began to rasp and break the lining next to his larynx.

Tuloki took his free hand and gripped the back of his head again, and while still gripping the hole puncher, slammed his fist down on his mouth twice." Shut the fuck up! You should've just given me those coordinates." Don, now bleeding from his mouth, began whiplashing his head as violently as possible, but Tuloki slammed his head back onto the headrest and pressed it with his forearm, to include the rest of his body weight to minimize Don's movement. He gripped the other eyelid and slid it into the hole puncher. This time he clamped down only twice, but manage to produce a larger figure-eight-type hole in the eyelid.

Don was coughing blood that was tricking down the back of his throat from his nose, and now was seeing a sea of blood as the capillaries on his eyelids drained out onto his face as well.

Blood leaked from his eyes, nose, and mouth.

The volume of blood loss had begun to total up, and Don began to feel lethargic. It didn't matter that he was nearly drowning in his own blood, or that he no longer had an escape strategy. He simply wanted to lay down and close his eyes. But...of course, that was no longer an option now.

His heavy head drooped down as Tuloki stepped away without uttering a word to him. He raised his eyes upward and noticed that his eyelids had been shut for a while now and that he had been looking through a new set of permanent holes. He tried to blink but the muscles that controlled his eyelids were no longer responsive. This was his new view of the world. This was his new reality.

CHAPTER 32

His new distorted perception was enough to make him aware of his surroundings, but he still second-guessed himself on what he was seeing. Besides being able to feel his pulse through his holey eyelids, and have tears being constantly produced, he still felt as if they were constantly drying out. He knew he couldn't open his eyes so he tried blinking them. The only thing he was able to manage was a scrunching of his forehead and eyebrows. His vision did narrow slightly, but never enough to be able to cover his pupils. He was constantly seeing what was in front of him, no matter how he attempted to roll or cover his eyeballs. He was still trying to manage the copious amount of blood that was leaking from different orifices of his face when he noticed that Tuloki had walked back to the table of tools where he went the first time.

This time he did not grab a set of tools immediately, but rather opened and shut drawers and tossed miscellaneous objects aside. Don was ready to admit to himself that fear had indeed risen within him. He could not imagine what type of new tormented way Tuloki was going to inflict pain on him. He was craving just a simple beat down versus having to experience whatever else Tuloki's imagination could muster.

Don was no longer swallowing what seemed to be an

open tap faucet of blood down his throat. He was still spitting out blood in between trying to clear his eyes and blow out through his nose. Tuloki had stopped opening draws and now began to look around the desk. He paused before crouching down and reached under the small gap that existed underneath the table. Out came a long pruning saw with rusted but sharp teeth. Don began to come to terms that he was going to lose an appendix when he noticed that Tuloki hadn't even glanced in his direction, but rather walked directly over to Elle. With a small flick of the wrist, Tuloki spewed dark smoke from his hands that connected with Elle's arm. Once he noticed that this was Elle's Wrist-Vector arm, he began to shout franticly.

"No!" Buried in denial, his first instinct was to just refuse the possibility that he would cut off her arm, but he immediately knew that Tuloki was set forth to carry out his original plan. "Wait! Just wait!" The pain-stricken pleads never re-routed a single step in Tuloki's direct path towards her. Without a single breath of hesitation, Tuloki grabbed her dark smoke levitated arm and placed the saw on her forearm, just a couple of inches under the bend of her elbow. He pressed it into her arm with increasing pressure, and once he broke skin and blood began to trickle out, he lifted his head and stared at Don, directly past his disfigured eyelids, and into his pupils. Despite the amount of blood that covered his facial features, it was still clearly noticeable that Don was frozen in disbelief and consumed with enormous guilt. Tuloki's arm grew in girth as his muscles flexed and began moving the saw forward. The teeth of the saw made quick work of Elle's skin layer. It only took about three single movements of the saw, and then it was starting to tear at the muscle fibers of her forearm.

Don shouted a tremendous scream that produced no coherent words. Tears filled his eyes and they mixed into the blood surrounding the corners of his face. "Nooooooo!" Don's neck veins pressed out of his neck and reverberate in place. What skin still remained visible began to flush red until both his blood and face nearly matched in color. "I'll give you the coordinates."

"I don't believe you!" Tuloki continued to saw at her arm, ripping muscle fiber and skin the deeper he went until he hit bone. Elle's limp body had begun to convulse as her arm began to spray bright red blood that was coming from her artery. It was only a matter of time before enough blood was spilled, that would never allow for Elle to regain her consciousness. Don could see how the saw slowed in movement and how Tuloki strained in the effort. It was clear to him that her arm had been more than half cut off, and it was also clear to him that he would do anything at this point to make him stop.

"I said I'll give you the codes! Please, just stop, and it's yours." A pause in saw movement occurred. However, the blood pouring around it had not. Tuloki glanced at the Wrist-Vector that was attached to Elle and noticed it was still activated.

"Go! You have mere seconds to give them to me! No messing with your device this time. You better remember that shit or we are done here. I'll plug it into her device, and if it reveals their location...then I'll go." Perhaps it was the excitement from the possibility of him actually, and finally learning the location toValeria. Or maybe it was the amount of focus required to keep Elle under his spell, Don's wrist bound, and physically attempt to cut through an arm with only a hand saw, but the smoke that was holding Don's hand together began to grow weaker. The dark mist encircling his hands cease rotating and loosened its constricting grip. There was more space in which he could move his wrists now, and he immediately took advantage.

Don tried to maintain his bearing intact. He did not want to divulge any sentiment that might clue Tuloki onto his lack of focus. He slowly slipped his right-hand loose and crawled his bloody fingers over the opposing wrist. With minute movements, he began to turn the dial of his Wrist-Vector. He had already preset his location on his previous attempt to call for backup, all that remained was for him to press onto the crystal sides of the glowing pyramid with his fingerprints, and wait to rescue to arrive in a matter of seconds. His thumb was the first finger to press onto the cold crystal. His forefinger and middle finger were next to press firmly onto the adjacent sides. He took a deep breath through his bleeding mouth and his muscles relaxed.

He had survived. He had survived long enough to relay a distress call.

"Continue to keep your tongue, Don, and she will lose her arm. Last chance. Tell me!"

Any moment now.

A team of Elites will arrive through the door and have him pinned down.

Any moment now...

Except there was a delay. No confirmation of successful signal sent. His muscle tightened once again. Stress and anxiety began to grow and seep into his cervical spine. Confused, he pressed firmly once again onto his Wrist-Vector. His fingers slipped off.

There was too much blood.

Fingerprint recognition could not be established.

With time completely sanded down, he instinctively wiped his hand on his shorts. He was certain that before blood trickled onto his fingertip again, he would be able to establish a proper connection. He was right, the blood had not yet begun to reach his fingertips.

Hope and calculated certainty flowed through him and his hand sped back towards his Wrist-Vector.

Then all hope was shattered.

"Mother Fucker!" Tuloki's mouth dropped, as did his brows in complete anger. "Your hands are free!" Tuloki had spotted his freed hand as he briefly wiped them on his shorts. Don was moving at quick speeds, as his mind was. With thought present, but mostly instincts taking over. He was completely zoned in on retrieving backup, he had forgotten to be stealthy with his free hand. As his heart sank with the weight of lead, he knew that this mistake would cost Elle's life. The anchoring of his heart falling into the pit of his stomach made him gag and almost vomit. He was dumbfounded at how completely moronic he had been to slip up in such an obvious way. His heavy heart clouded his mind and restricted his movements. "Every chance I had given you today has been completely tossed aside. A waste! You and yours are just a fucking waste. This next and final stage of Elle's life will be unequivocally and completely your fault. I want you to know that...but I can see you already do."

Tuloki raised both his hands above Elle's body, closed his eyes, and chanted once again in an indiscernible tongue. They syllables spoken were short and fierce. The longer her continued the faster he spoke. His words became faster and fiercer. The dark mist that once covered most of her body started to thin out until it dissipated completely into the surrounding space.

He had completely removed his spell over her and her consciousness. Without another moment of hesitation, he grabbed the hand saw, jammed it into her wound. He began to heave as he expelled great force and energy into sawing her arm. He did not let up the intensity of his forceful swings as he ripped through bone and tissue. He never slowed down, not even when Elle's eyes shot open.

CHAPTER 33

The sound that came out of Elle's mouth immediately sank Don's heart until it laid flat against his diaphragm. The ear-splitting shrill of a cry pounded against his eardrum and sent a jolt of pain that he felt go down along his throat. Goosebumps raised along the back of his neck and continued up into his scalp.

Elle started screaming even before her eyes focused on her new surroundings. The sheer pain that she had to awaken to, placed her in such a state of shock that after her initial scream was complete, she began gasping for air in short intervals. She grabbed at her throat, and at her other arm that was on the brink of being sawed completely off. Her body was incredibly weak and made no significant trouble in slowing down Tuloki's sawing arm. Her body twisted and wrangled like she was undergoing a demonic exorcism. Her left arm had no longer twitched as the rest of her body did. Enough muscles and nerves had been severed that it no longer participated with any of her cognitive responses.

Tuloki stood up while gripping onto her wrists with both of his hands, placed his foot in the pocket of her shoulder, and began to pull with all his strength. His bent knee fully extended as he yanked his hands towards his chest. There was an obvious connection still between arm and body as he strained his back even further to accomplish his goal. With another jerk backward that involved the coordination of his entire body, Elle's forearm was pulled, yanked, and ultimately, ripped off like a chicken wing at a weekend barbeque.

Tuloki's lower half of his body was drenched in her blood, meanwhile, his upper body had nothing but Don's blood. He rose with her forearm in hand and began to pace towards him. Elle once again began to scream in anguish as she watched her arm become separated from her body. She made eye contact with Don for a moment and all that was displayed was confusion and utter fear. The brief moment in time that their eyes met sparked a rage inside of him that caused him to scream out in fury.

"Nooooooo!" His voice echoed through the warehouse and was only muffled by the continuous screams being ranged from Elle's mouth. She began to choke on her saliva that was spurting out and was now in a dangerous fight between losing oxygen and bleeding out from her arm.

Tuloki reached within a couple of feet of where Don was still bound to the chair and leap forward with one foot in front. His heel made contact square on his chest sending him backward, chair and all. As his body was about to meet the ground, he let out another yell. His voice ignited his other senses and time appeared to slow down. He noticed while still falling that in his rage, he no longer felt any pain. His vision was narrowed, but clear. His hands still bleeding but clenched. His breath quickened and his mind was focused with stricken purpose. It was due to his heightened senses, that when Don's body did hit the metal tiles underneath him, he heard a sound that would be his last hope of survival. As his body crashed onto the ground, all the items in his gear belt subsequentially came tumbling out, and out from his boot, fell out Chris's Ahir Blade. The clink-a-clank it created sent a note of reminder directly into his brain, and it brought him some much-needed focus. He knew if he could get his hand on it, and be able to spring out the blade at just the right moment, he might be able to reach Elle in time to save her.

He was still in an awkward position and unable to move his body much. His hands were unbounded but his elbows, torso, and legs still were. He could feel the blade that had dropped from his boot resting against his hip, but he was unable to reach for it with ease. His arms, still mostly bound at the elbows behind the chair, had been crushed by fall and had the weight of his body on top of them. He was face up, body squared off to the ceiling, but still trying to inch over to the blade. He was but an inch or two away from being able to fully grasp the handle, but it was lodged between the chair and floor. He could feel the handle with his fingertips, and he continued to attempt to release it, but it was secured and immovable. He rocked his torso back and forth to try and levitate his hips, removing some of that weight compressed onto the blade, but Tuloki came and ceased those efforts.

He placed his boot on Don's neck and applied pressure. He stood directly above him and looked down his nose at him. He held tight onto Elle's arm and it hovered over his stomach, dripping warm blood. Standing there with a smug look on his face, he began to shake his head in distaste. "You imbecile. You could have lived the rest of your miserable life with that one-armed bitch over there, but you just would not listen. You could not wrap your mind around the fact that you've been lied to about everything Valeriahas been feeding you." Tuloki leaned his body weight forward, and Don felt every pound of added pressure. "Now you'll die here under the heel of my boot, and all for nothing." Every pound of pressure on his neck was another minute of life that was quickly fleeting from him. Yet, he wanted more, needed more pressure on his neck.

Don felt as if his Adam's apple was about to be crushed into his spine. His narrowed airway strained his neck to inhale whatever air as possible, and yet through this, he pushed his efforts into speaking. "You...you are..." Don began to cough and wheeze. Tuloki's smug grew even larger and his peaked interest led him to lift his booth only enough to hear what Don had to say. Another desperate breath managed to scarcely fill his lungs enough to speak again. "You're just so pathetic"

Tuloki's raised eyebrow of curiosity quickly lowered and angled into a deep angry frown. He snarled with a trembling rage. He realigned his foot and placed all his weight onto it this time. Don immediately began to see black and grey spots in what vision he had left. There was a small crunch as the cartilage from his Adam's apple snapped. Don snarled back at Tuloki while staring him right in the eye. Slowly more teeth showed and his snarl turned into a grin. Tuloki began to twist his heel and his thigh muscles began to twitch due to the added muscle pressure being applied. The more pressure that was applied to his throat, the more Don grinned. The more Don grinned, the more Tuloki expelled effort into crushing his neck. This vicious cycle could only go on for seconds longer, and Don knew that. However, that wasn't the math he was focused on. He was only focused on the simple physics required to lift his hip and chair up enough to free the blade. What he needed was for Tuloki to pressed on his neck further, rocking the entire chair back just enough to release the wedged blade. Not the pain, nor the lack of oxygen mattered any longer. He knew this was his only route to save Elle.

His fingers continued to strain and pull at the handle relentlessly. He thought if maybe he had all of his full fingers, just maybe, he would have been able to grip better, he also started to think about purple bunnies painting waterfalls on the sides of brick buildings.

Hallucinations started to enter his mind due to the lack of oxygen and blood traveling to his brain. He recognized these signs and had to ensure his focus did not falter any further. It was at that moment where he felt the blade give a little. This was all the hope needed to restore his focus.

The last of Don's teeth were revealed in his ultimate grin.

The last of Tuloki's physical strength was used to push into his body.

The last of pressure compressing the blade was lifted, and the blade was finally freed.

Don nailed at the handle until he was able to grip it fully. He rotated his wrist and angled the blade towards the ropes that bound his elbows. He compressed his fingers to initiate the blade release, and the swift metal sliced through the rope releasing his arms fully. He used what strength remained, and fueled it with his anger to simultaneously rip his arms from out under the chair. He cupped his left hand and swung it around towards the back of the leg that was on his neck. With the momentum of his arm swing, he grabbed onto the back of his knee and yanked it forward, instantly causing it to buckle. Tuloki, having all his weight on that leg, came tumbling down head first, and was headed to fall right on top of Don. In a singular swift motion, Don darted his hand forward and thrust the blade into the jugular of Tuloki's neck.

Don was holding the entire weight of Tuloki's body on that blade. His right arms were shaking while attempting to balance the blade and the body it was in. It was jammed so far into his neck that the tip of the sacred Ahir Blade protruded from the back of his neck. Don was breathing heavy, anger was still consuming him, and even though he knew no one could survive what he had just done, he had to see it through. It was the first time that he had ever ended a life. He stared into the emptying eyes of the soon-to-be corpse on top of him.

There wasn't much left in there, and the longer he stared the more he could see his own bleeding face in its reflection. Tuloki's left eye, the one closest to his neck wound, began to cloud. Dark black lines scrawled across the whites of his eye and grew thicker. Don traced their origins and saw that they led towards the side of his face. There too, were dark black lines slivering over mottled grey skin. The roots of this growing darkness were found to be pooling out from a grey smoke that surrounded the blade, and the deep wound it created. The same mystic smoke that Tuloki generated earlier, was now purging out of Don's own hand.

He could feel it seeping out of his pores. He felt a connection to it, and a power tied directly to it too. He felt the raw energy waiting for instructions as it hovered around his hand and the blade. Then, before any other notions were conceived, Don, or the smoke, or perhaps the both of them combined, twisted the blade that was lodge in Tuloki's neck, and then ripped it out sideways through his cervical spine. A mist of blood and smoke filled the air around them as Tuloki's head was severed, and all that remained what the Ahir Blade in the sky. The headless corpse thumped on the ground next to Don, and he didn't bother to even look at its remnants as he stood up.

CHAPTER 34

His eye caught the slowly breathing body of Elle that laid armless in the ground no more than 50 feet away. Her life was depleting right in front of him and he worried if he still had enough time. He bent down and grabbed Elle's severed arm. It was still gripped by a stiff grasp and had to pry it out from the fingers of this dead stranger who had now changed him forever. He limped over to her and immediately began applying an improvised tourniquet. He turned the cloth and stick until the bleeding stopped and lean in to listen to her laborious breathing.

"Elle....baby, please don't quit on me." He began stroking her hair. "It's over, it's done. We can go home." His voice was raspy and barely over a whisper. His recently compressed throat has led to a painful speech, still, he had to speak to her. Tears began to fall alongside his cheek and drop onto the ground next to her, leaving a light pink splatter from the blood it collected along the way. He checked her pulse from her remaining arm only to find that it was barely there. From the wounds they both sustained, Don knew that they were meant to die there, and he thought that they still might. Elle turned to face him and opened her mouth.

No words came out.

All she could muster was to place her hand on his and look him in the eye. If it was not for Elle making eye contact with him, he might have stayed there holding her until they both passed away. But it was in the energy from her gaze that he found the strength to not only stand up but pick her up over his shoulders. Next would come his next mystery. Once he walked out the doors of that warehouse, he knew not how far the distance would be to the door leading back to Joshua Hills Waypoint. All that was outside that warehouse seemed to be a distant memory. He wasn't even sure he if would have the mental capabilities to return to the Waypoint, but remaining there was no option either.

To further mock him in his distress, the moment he stepped outside, his Wrist-Vector alarm activated, signaling that he had but five minutes to cross over before remaining stuck there. He contemplated requesting emergency backup, but he knew that reconfiguring his request and lock in coordinates, would take longer than he had. He pushed on the door with his shoulder and fought the outside wind for control. He thought the last of his energy would finally be expelled right then and there. It was only once he gained the advantage and managed to open the door fully, that he then realized he would surely lose his energy walking in this newfound atmosphere. The wind he just fought was not unaccompanied. It trekked along with think globes of snow. As each colony of snowflakes landed on him, they instantly melted and transferred into steam rising from his overheated body.

Only one thing remained in his favor, and that was that he had visual confirmation of where the remaining door stood. He could see it off in the distance, solid, unlike his shaking legs. His heavy head lowered as he began to endure his journey there. All he could see was his feet rise a lower as drops of blood painted the snow on the ground like a single-color Pollock painting. Each step reminded him of two things, the first was the possibility of imminent death due to the excruciating pain that now infiltrated almost every square inch of his body. This excruciating pain was directly connected to not only his life, but to the precious creature, he was carrying. Secondly, the mystery that was clouding the forefront of his mind as it clouded his hands just moments ago. He needed to know what was that dark energy that was emanating from not only Tuloki but himself as well. As much as he wanted to deny his involvement with that consuming smoke, he could not lie to himself and make pretend as if he still didn't feel its lingering presence. He recalled a time where he once could validate all his teachings and knowledge directly to its source, but he was no longer certain. This uncertainty and unremovable desire for knowledge propelled him to dig deeper and drive every step further and faster. His increase in speed created more pain as his breath became even more labored. Each inhalation felt like he was swallowing scolding hot razor blades. He tried to hold his breath, but that only lead to an even larger breath immediately following the underwhelming short moment of relief.

His busy mind came to a crashing halt when he lifted his head and could no longer see the door.

"Shit, it happened." The doors crawled, babe." He didn't even notice when it did. He didn't even know if Elle was still alive. He began to question if he was even alive at this point and had just been walking in some sort of snowy purgatory all along. "I'm sorry... I'm so—" A dedicated gust of wind turned his body around and had his face to face with the Waypoint door. He thought himself a fool to had given up so easily. Before another thought entered his mind, he reached the doorknob and collapsed into the doorway.

His body hit the ground of the dusty and patchy grass he never knew he could miss so much. He heard the tumble of Elle right in front of him and couldn't help but smile as he realized they had both made it through. Just then, his boot popped off his foot and was being dragged away. He quickly pulled his leg into his stomach and looked down to his feet. They had crossed the doorway with only a few seconds to spare. The door they just came from, and all the doors around them began to crawl into new positions. His foot just happened to be in the way of this door's particular new path. He relaxed his body and allowed himself to melt into the ground.

His smile became more prominent as he smelled again the earth he was laying on. The familiar landscape of the place he called home all these years, was once again an aroma he could taste. More importantly and surprisingly so, it was not the smell of blood. Nor was he now tasting it. He pushed himself up with his hands, which were now not only bloodless but fully intact. There was a slightly darker tint on the finger that was previously mauled, but they were complete as he remembered them. He rubbed his thumbs along his fingertips and was pleased to feel all the sensations with no pain. He rushed his hands to his eyelids but already realized they too were back to normal as he blinked them shut over and over again. "No holes!" His emotions began to resurface as his body return to homeostasis.

He took a couple of steps over to where Elle was beginning to move around again. She moaned and groaned as she sat herself up. She looked over to him, where he stood looking strangely pleased. Pleased of course with the fact that she had her arm rightfully intact, with a darker shade also, but completely there. Elle glanced down at her arm and began to massage it.

"Was...all that real?" Don crouched down in front of her and grabbed the sides of her face with both his hands. He leaned his head in and placed his forehead on hers.

"Very real I'm afraid. But it's no longer a reality of ours." He kissed the side of her cheek and wiped away a tear that glided down her face.

"I remember a lot of it, but I can't place it into words. I'm a little scared and a little in pain, but I feel so good too. So alive." She massaged her arm again and looked up at him. "How?"

"Your arm? We are not part of that realm anymore. The DNA changes that occurred while we were across the door were sufficient enough to make us more part of that world than ours. Although there were many similarities in our biological structures, there were enough to cause a complete return to self as we returned." He took his finger and traced his eyelids, and then her arm where she was cut before. "Still, it appears that enough of the trauma remained that it has permanently altered our skin. And thankfully so, because now we will never forget."

Elle took her fingers and ran them across her arm, ensuring that what she was feeling was indeed her arm. She looked at Don and then ran her fingertips across his eyelids. "I remember seeing you with your eyes—"

"It's okay, Elle. I'm okay now."

"What about that guy? Is he...dead?"

"I believe so. I don't know how to explain it but..." He paused for a moment as he glanced over to the crawling doors, realizing that even if he wanted to return, he had no idea where the door went. "When I heard you screaming, and I witnessed you in all that pain and suffering...I knew. I just knew that I was going to kill him."

They remained there, kneeling next to each other for a

while longer, embracing each other in silence. Either it all had to be discussed, or none of it did. They both felt exhausted and drained and agreed they would much rather return home.

CHAPTER 35

No dreams and no thoughts were had by either of them that night. Their bodies laid in stillness as both mind and physical body were being repaired. The outside air had sensed their return and greeted them back with an endless caress of soothing winds. Their slumber was not once interrupted, and when they woke, they had a newfound appreciation for each other, the breath they inhaled, and all things surrounding them. Only Don remained with a gauge needing to be filled, and questions to be answered. He did not know what else was out there for him, but he knew he had to attempt to find out.

He was the second to awaken, Elle had already been downstairs, and from the smell of it, cooking. His wounds from the day prior were no longer physically there, but their existence still was partially present as he felt an overall soreness. He gradually stepped down the stairs and was making a conscious effort to take his sweet time with most things. He wanted to soak in each moment of peace and tranquility for as long as possible until it was time for him to go seek his answers.

When he reached the last step, he held his movement momentarily as he starred at Elle and took in this visual input for the magnificent sight that it was. The woman he loved was safe, and so was he. No one would have known the journey of their previous day, and no one would ever need to. This bubble of theirs was beautiful the way it was. Neither one of them knew it at the time, but those next moments, was as normal as their bubble will ever be.

"I smell something familiar, babe." Don stepped down the final step and joined her in the kitchen.

"Just something Dayna showed me one night after I asked her. I know it's your favorite." She grinned and popped him a quick kiss on the cheek.

"No. Is it really?" He sidestepped to get around her, looked at the pot, and threw his hands in the air. "Oh, hell yeah! It's her 10-Cheese Mac-N-Cheese with bacon and scallions." He jammed out to a tune in his head that he hummed out loud while grooving his hips and finger guns side to side. It didn't take too long after that until they were both at the table eating and conversating in harmony.

The clanks of the forks and clunks of the cups were the only sounds he wanted to hear for a long time, but he knew Elle, and he knew she had things on her mind. She took a sip from her glass of his homemade moonshine after completing her last bite. She savored the completion of her meal and relished in the silence. She looked up at him and said nothing. Don knew it was time to think again, to plan again. "What now?" Elle asked.

"Excuse me?" Elle didn't respond to him, simply raised an eyebrow. Don wanted to tell her everything that happened, and everything that Tuloki had said. He wanted to tell her about all the questions he had on his and how they were tormenting his mind. He especially wanted to tell her about the black smoke that came from his rage. He wanted, but he did not know where to start. Elle was about to make that starting point a lot more specific for him.

"Are you going to ask me to stay? Or after everything we been through, are you still not going to ask?" Don wasn't prepared for that question. He never really considered not being next to her as he tried to figure out this new mystery that was plaguing his every other thought. He also never really imagined that her life would have been in such danger. There was new information here that he was learning, which seem to directly lead to new dangers. "Just say something, instead of thinking it all in your head. I'm here, right in front of you. For now." She stood up and grabbed both their plates. "When I come back with thirds, I want an answer" She looked at him with a held gaze before she walked away to the kitchen.

Don's head ignited into a fury of imaginative formulas with even a larger number of crazed variables. He saw all the good and all the bad that would come from him asking her to stay. He did not want to make the bad call, but he also didn't know how to come up with the right answer. He thought it should be up to her. He closed his eyes and drew in deep breathes. He searched his dark eyes for any clues of his feelings. He searched his feeling for any clues of his mind. He knew he could spend the rest of the day, and week possibly not making a decision. He almost just wanted to flip a coin. The only thing he did know is that he wanted to see her ace again.

"Stay," Don said out loud. "Please stay, I mean, if you want."

There was no response from Elle. He thought she was not satisfied with the way he asked. Afterall, he wasn't too convinced himself. He decided it was time to mean it, for he truly did want her to stay.

"Stay!"

No response.

"I want you to stay."

No response.

"C'mon, I've said it. I want you to stay. Will you?"

With yet still no response, Don did not want to wait any longer and stood up and went directly to her for a response. Except, she was not there. Don looked back to the table where they were just eating and did not see her there either. He shook his head at his brainless response to not being in the kitchen as if she just walked by him without him noticing. So, he then became confused about where she was but was distracted by a big blue note that was left on the counter. He read it:

"Don, I'm staying! I don't care if you ask or not anymore. We started something here, and I'm staying to see it through. P.S. Come find me before the doors crawl."
– XOXO Elle

Don put the note down and looked through the window. There she was, the woman he loved, running into the unknown, ready for anything, and he would be there too. Right by her side…for as long as the realms and time allowed.

THE END

Made in the USA
Middletown, DE
10 September 2021